TRAIL OF PROMISES

THE GREAT WAGON ROAD
BOOK TWO

SUSAN F. CRAFT

WILD HEART
BOOKS

ISBN-13: 978-1-942265-96-2

PRAISE FOR TRAIL OF PROMISES

"Craft deftly balances high-intensity action with moments of genuine heart. This is swoonworthy."

— PUBLISHERS WEEKLY

"Carefully researched and beautifully written, *Trail of Promises* is the charming story of two young people brought together by tragedy, yet bound together by the hope of a new and better life. While author Susan Craft doesn't shy away from the very real hardships and dangers faced by our country's earliest settlers, she tempers her tale with the very best of the human spirit: resilience, fortitude, faith, and love. For readers of historical romance, this is one story you don't want to miss."

— ANN TATLOCK, NOVELIST, EDITOR, WRITING MENTOR

"*Trail of Promises* offers an amazing glimpse into the early settlers in the South. Their hardships and losses, as well as their ability to recover and move forward, speaks volumes about the stamina and grit that was needed to form these United States.

In the midst of one young woman's grief, a love is born that is then threatened by unexpected evil. Can the tender Tessa, inexperienced in the ways of the wilderness, survive the threats to her happiness and her future?"

— ELAINE MARIE COOPER, AUTHOR,
SCARRED VESSELS AND THE *DAWN OF AMERICA SERIES*

To my granddaughter, McKenzie, an amazingly talented and gifted artist. She reads her subjects' emotions and portrays them on canvas in a way that grabs her audiences and inspires them to feel those emotions. Her portraits and sketches cover my office walls. Her creations surround me and fill me with awe. I love you, dear one.

INTRODUCTION

The Great Wagon Road spanned from Philadelphia, Pennsylvania, through Virginia, North Carolina, and South Carolina and ended in Augusta, Georgia. It began as a path carved out of the wilderness by thousands of bison and deer moving from one water source and salt lick to the next. Indians used the footpath for hunting and for warring against neighboring tribes. Hernando de Soto is reported to have trekked part of the trail during his exploration of the Southeast in the 1500s. Europeans, many of them landed gentry, made new fortunes trapping deer and selling the hides along the road. In the 1700s, the road expanded into a major thoroughfare traveled by immigrants, a large number of them Scots-Irish. Colonel George Washington and his troops traversed the road during the French and Indian War. Over time, the Great Wagon Road had many names. Among them were Great Warriors' Trail, Indian Road, and Valley Pike.

Come, journey with Tessa Harris, a portrait artist, and Stephen Griffith, a former British cavalry officer, as they bestow upon the Great Wagon Road a new name, *Trail of Promises*.

INTRODUCTION

CHAPTER 1

JUNE 15, 1753

Strolling alongside her family's covered wagon through a dense forest with more trees than she could name, Tessa Harris dragged a stick across weeds that draped onto the edges of the trail. Though it was only early morning, the air already sweltered, and she welcomed the tufts of mist that moistened her arms. The emotional burden she carried weighed her down as heavily as the humidity.

Today marked her nineteenth birthday as well as the second anniversary of her mother's death. Both had passed without mention. Had her mother been alive, she would have awakened Tessa with laughter and a silly ditty. Name day presents and cakes would have awaited her at the breakfast table.

A gray rabbit thrashed through a nearby bush and scurried so close to her toes, she hopped back. She dropped the stick and adjusted the strap of the rucksack slung over her shoulder. The canvas bag held her sketchbook, charcoal, and pencils. She never allowed it far from her reach.

Her father, Thomas Harris, drove their wagon with the ease born of many years' experience as a limner traveling from town to town seeking commissions for portraits. But his tall, lean form hunched on the bench. Last night's drinking had left his usually handsome face bloated and his mood testy.

She moved closer to the wagon. "Father?"

"What is it?" he snapped. He did not look at her but concentrated on the team of horses.

Should she engage with him or let him be? Despite his moroseness, she missed his companionship.

"How far have we come since leaving Philadelphia?"

He continued looking ahead. "Around a hundred miles."

"So three hundred more to go?"

He grumbled and jerked the reins. "Give or take."

His terseness precluded any further conversation. Tessa walked on in silence until they reached a section of the trail so narrow it caused her to squeeze closer to the wagon. Her father angrily shoved away a pine branch that threatened to slap his face. The brim of his black felt hat flopped over his forehead as if to shelter his stoic expression and the grief lines etched on either side of his mouth.

He abruptly pulled back on the reins, bringing the wagon to a halt. "Tessa, you'll have to take over."

Tessa's spirits slumped.

"Why have you stopped, Miss Harris? Is something wrong?" a voice called out behind her.

She turned as Stephen Griffith, the owner of the wagon that followed hers, prodded his coal-black stallion toward her. The master and his horse made a striking picture.

"Good morning." She curtsied.

During their short acquaintance, they had made only fleeting, casual conversation, but his engaging smile that lit his eyes and his friendly manner appealed to her. Her pulse fluttered each time he came near.

"It's my father. He's unwell and I must drive." Avoiding his gaze, she concentrated on pulling the worn leather gloves from her belt and slipping them on.

Mr. Griffith dismounted, stroked his horse's jaw, and murmured, "My fine Knight." The horse nuzzled his shoulder before Mr. Griffith looked up at her.

"One of my brothers would be happy to drive for you. Although Francis and Adam have both become proficient this past week, they quarrel over who will drive. You would be doing me a favor by allowing one of them to assist you."

"That's kind of you, but I can manage. Father and I traveled many miles as we moved from one commission to the next, and I often drove our wagon." She chuckled. "I got quite good at dodging holes in the road, especially in remote country villages."

Without acknowledging Mr. Griffith's presence, her father slapped the reins around the brake and climbed inside the wagon.

His rudeness mortified her. "Do forgive my father—"

Mr. Griffith stepped closer to her. "Please, there's no need to apologize."

He was so tall, Tessa had to lean back to gaze into his warm brown eyes.

No, not just brown. Sienna. Burnt sienna.

Considered individually, each of his features was unremarkable. A square jaw covered by a cropped dark-brown beard. Long nose. Full lips shadowed by a thin mustache. Dark, feathery eyebrows that framed his golden-brown eyes. And curly sable-brown hair he wore loose, flowing over his ears and resting on his collar. Taken all together, though, his was a handsome, arresting face. Although his arms, exposed by his rolled-up sleeves, were tanned from many hours in the sun, Tessa could tell that his complexion was naturally pale.

He cleared his throat. "Is something amiss?"

Tessa blinked and flushed over being caught staring. "Oh, do forgive me. I tend to get lost studying people. Have you ever had your portrait done?"

"Me? No. Definitely not. My younger brothers said you allowed them to see samples of your work. You're brilliant, according to them."

She fiddled with the strap of her rucksack. The two young men had shown genuine interest in her work. "What a nice thing to hear."

He glanced up the trail at the cloud of dust stirred by the last wagon that had rounded the bend. "Let's not let the others get too far ahead."

He slipped the rucksack from her shoulder, clasped her elbow, and helped her up onto the wagon seat.

Tessa wrinkled her nose at the knee-high cloud of dust already lingering in the air. Today, hers and Mr. Griffith's wagons were the last in line. The farther the train ventured during the day, the higher the dust cloud would grow.

"You have a kerchief?" he asked and handed her the rucksack.

"I do." Tessa reached into the side slit of her petticoats and pulled her scarf from her under-pocket. "Thank you for your kindness."

She waited for Mr. Griffith to step back before slapping the reins and driving the horses forward. Closing the gap that had formed behind the previous wagon, she fought the misgivings that crowded her thoughts. How could she manage if her father persisted in his drinking? Driving the wagon, settling down each evening with the eight other families, building a fire, cooking the meal, caring for the horses, and preparing the bedrolls underneath the wagon exhausted her so much that she often retired without speaking a word to anyone. Some nights, too spent to sleep, she lit a candle and worked on her sketches.

Carrying the burden of their family drained her mentally. She needed her father. A master portrait artist, at one time, he had charmed his female subjects, perusing them with his intense cobalt-blue eyes that delved into their personalities, bringing them to life on canvas. His wife's death had cast a pall over his artistic passion. Drink had doused the fire in his eyes.

When their ship docked in Philadelphia weeks prior, Tessa had hoped the adventure of a wagon train and the promise of a new portrait studio in the South Carolina colony would lift his spirits, but the opposite held true. His moods swung between anger and melancholy with increasingly rare expressions of more tender emotions between.

Did her father not see how his behavior frightened her? How alone she felt, uprooted from everything familiar and dropped into a world of strangers and sights and sounds so alien from their home in England?

Her prayers had become fervent pleas for her old father to return to her.

How sad to compare what was real with what she wished life to be. Even so, she had to put on a brave face. And one day, she'd see her father smile again.

A deer bounded from the woods and streaked across the trail, startling the lead horse. It reared up and gave out a scream that sounded almost human.

Tessa pulled back on the reins with all her might as the wagon rocked back and forth. A loud *crack* and the wagon careened to the side. She shrieked as she was tossed into the air.

CHAPTER 2

Stephen had not ridden far toward his wagon when the Harrises' horse screamed. He swung Knight around and rushed alongside Miss Harris just as she tumbled off the seat. He circled his arm around her waist, lifted her onto his horse, and tucked her close to him.

She was as light as a feather. Almost fragile, barely reaching his shoulder when they stood side by side. The kind of woman a man would desire to protect. Her soft, warm body curled naturally into his. Wisps of her corn-silk-colored hair had escaped her mobcap and framed her oval face. Light-blue smudges colored the skin beneath her eyes. The week on the wagon train had taken its toll, but she had grit, proven with the way she handled not only the team of horses but her drunkard of a father.

She splayed her hand across his chest. Could she feel his heart hammering from her delicate touch?

"Are you hurt?" he asked, looking down at her fingers.

"No. But my father!"

Stephen had forgotten the man. He carefully lowered her to the ground, dismounted, and hurried to the back of the wagon.

She rushed after him and waited until he assisted the disheveled man onto the ground. Then she clasped her father around his waist and buried her face in his chest.

Mr. Harris gently pushed Tessa away and held her by her shoulders. "All is well. Don't fret, my dear." He kissed the top of his daughter's head before nodding at Stephen. "Thank you, sir. I'm in your debt."

Stephen bowed his head. "I'm thankful I could help." At least the man still possessed some manners. And some tenderness for his daughter.

Stephen studied Tessa's face as she struggled to hide her distress. She pulled in a deep breath and let it out slowly as she focused on the toes of her shoes.

Francis and Adam came running so fast they barely missed crashing into her. Several years apart, they were handsome boys with dark hair, brown eyes, and open, honest expressions.

Francis, who was the same height as Tessa, retrieved her mobcap from the ground, handed it to her, and searched her eyes. "You all right, Miss Harris?"

She brushed out the folds in her petticoats and shook the dirt from her mobcap. "Thanks to your brother, I am." She hooked a stray curl behind her ear.

"Boys," said Stephen, "go see to Mr. Harris's horses. Check that none were hurt, especially the lead horse. He reared up and may have cut himself on the harness. And try to keep them calm."

"What of our canvases? The artwork?" Tessa moved toward the backboard.

Stephen clasped her elbow. "Don't get too close. The wheel might go entirely and collapse everything."

Mr. Harris peered into the wagon. "Doesn't look as though there's any damage inside. Everything is secure in crates, except our personal belongings that are in chests. They were tossed about a bit, though."

Stephen examined the wagon wheel. "Not the same here. It's damaged beyond repair."

Horse hooves approached, and Stephen turned as Sam Washburn, the wagon master, galloped toward them and halted beside their wagon.

"Anyone hurt?" Mr. Washburn asked.

In his fifties, the wagon master spryly dismounted and quickly approached them, despite a slight limp in his step. His hair, beard, and bushy eyebrows were the same mottled gray hues against his weather-beaten, deeply lined face.

Stephen shook his head. "The Harrises are fine. The axle wasn't damaged, but they'll need a new wheel."

Mr. Washburn tipped his hat toward Tessa. "Can't stop the train. We've about an hour before we reach our designated campsite." He inspected the broken wheel and scanned the trail and surrounding woods. "Trail is too narrow for you to get your wagon past, Mr. Griffith."

Stephen folded his arms across his chest. "I wouldn't leave them, anyway."

Some of the panic left Tessa's face. Did his presence mean safety for her?

Mr. Washburn ran his thumb and forefinger across his chin, removed his sweat-stained hat, and slapped it against his thigh. "The trees and underbrush are too thick to pull the wagon off to the side." He faced Tessa and her father. "Here's what we'll do. I'll get the train settled in. Several of the wagoners are carrying extra wheels. I'll send our scout back here with a wheel and some tools."

Mr. Harris offered his hand. "Thank you, Mr. Washburn. I regret the inconvenience."

The wagon master shook his hand. "It's fortunate that no one was injured." He mounted his horse and leaned his elbow on its neck. "These things happen. In the meantime, it's best if you unharness the horses and let them graze. You might want to shore up the side of that wagon bed, to be on the safe side. We wouldn't want it to fall on anyone." He wound the reins around his hand and turned his horse. "Build a fire and get some supper. It'll be dark before we get back to you. And don't be anxious, little lady. I promise, everything will be set back to rights soon."

Tessa nodded and lifted her chin in a show of bravery, but the trusting glance she turned on Stephen after the wagon master departed stirred him.

~

*D*espite Mr. Washburn's reassurances, Tessa's chest tightened as he rode away and headed up the trail. The reassuring smile Mr. Griffith offered her helped.

He and his brothers unhitched the draft horses. They attached them to a tether line in a small grassy clearing on the other side of a thick stand of pine trees. Mr. Griffith built a fire in the middle of the trail, and after bracing the side of the wagon, he allowed the boys to crawl in and out helping Tessa gather pots and supplies.

Next to the fire, Tessa perched on the edge of one of the chairs she and her father had brought with them. Her father drooped onto the other chair several feet away, a tankard of whiskey balanced on his lap. Mr. Griffith sat close to her on a stool and stretched out his long legs, digging the heels of his boots into the sand. The boys settled down cross-legged on a blanket.

Holding the cloth-covered handle of a frying pan in one hand, Tessa flipped a dollop of batter with a spatula and laid slabs of bacon along the sides of the pan. "Sorry, it's only corn-cakes and bacon."

"We have foodstuff—flour, sugar, potatoes..." Mr. Griffith offered.

Tessa brushed ashes from the hem of her petticoats. "For now, let's have this. We'll talk about combining supplies later."

"Yes, ma'am." He saluted.

"Oh, dear. Am I giving orders?"

"With good reason." He winked. "You are our quartermaster."

Charming man. And such a nice smile.

She continued cooking, trying to stay as far away from the fire as possible. The weather was scorching, leaving stains on the underarms of her bodice. Sweat beaded on her upper lip. The bacon needed a few more minutes, but she had to cool off. She put the frying pan on a flat rock beside the coals and retrieved a fan from her rucksack. She fluttered it, lifting strands of sweat-drenched hair that had escaped from her waist-length braid.

Francis sniffed the air and closed his eyes. "Food smells grand, Miss Harris."

"Why don't you, all of you, call me Tessa? It seems unnecessary, in our circumstances, to stand on ceremony."

Would Father approve of this lapse in propriety? Slumped in his chair, detached from everything around him, not even hiding his drinking, did he even care?

"Tessa, it is." Mr. Griffith straightened. "And call me Stephen."

The new level of intimacy made her eager to feel the sound of his name on her lips.

Stephen picked up the leather canteen next to his feet, pulled out the cork stopper, lifted the canteen, and guzzled the contents. Water drizzled down his neck and into the chest hair exposed by his open collar. Dragging her eyes away, Tessa fluttered her fan against her face.

"Francis, Adam, take the canteens from our wagon as well as two buckets and fill them from the creek just over there."

Stephen swept his arm toward the clearing where the horses grazed.

Tessa poked several strips of bacon with the spatula. "Don't take too long, though. Supper will be ready in a few minutes."

The boys raced away, chattering loudly in the distance.

She stacked a few of the cakes onto a plate. "They are fine young men, Stephen. How old are they?"

He pulled a pistol from his belt and set it on the ground by his feet. "Francis is sixteen and Adam is fourteen."

She turned over a sizzling slice of bacon, and a spot of grease landed on her hand. "Ouch!"

Stephen quickly pulled a kerchief from his waistcoat and wiped away the grease. He held her hand and examined the red mark, running his thumb across her skin. "Nothing serious."

What a contrast between his tan fingers and her pale ones. He let go of her, and she missed their warmth and strength.

She leaned down and picked up a couple of plates that lay on the blanket. "If you don't mind my asking, what of your parents?"

"Not at all. My father died four years ago, and my mother two years ago."

"My mother died two years ago also." Tessa glanced at her father, who had remained silent during the conversation. But he was listening, for he downed another drink of whiskey at the mention of death.

Stephen shook his head. "Something sad we have in common."

Tessa plated the food and handed one serving to Stephen and one to her father, who set his tankard on the ground. He was eating. What a relief.

"It can't have been easy bringing up two active boys."

"I can take no credit. I am Francis's senor by nine years and was away in the army...in India...when my mother died. Even though I had served the required years, it took me the better part of a year to give up my commission and settle my affairs. The boys stayed with a neighbor while I traveled back home." He sighed heavily. "They suffered a great deal, I'm afraid."

Her father put down the bacon he was about to eat. "India? Were you at Mumbai?"

Stephen turned his head away. "I was."

Tessa cocked her head. The memory troubled him. How many battles had he fought in? Many, if his air of quiet confidence was any indication.

Father jostled his plate on his lap. "Tessa, it was an infamous confrontation, but our British troops prevailed despite being outnumbered. Our losses were dreadful, though."

Stephen folded a corncake around a couple of pieces of bacon and took a bite. "Umm. So good."

He swallowed, downed the bite with water, and then raised two fingers to his lips, letting out a shrill whistle. One of the boys responded with a similar signal.

Minutes later, they came hobbling down the trail lugging the filled canteens and buckets. Once they had settled on the blanket, Tessa served them, and they pounced on the food. It vanished in seconds.

Francis wiped his mouth with the back of his hand. "Mighty good, Tessa."

"It was." Stephen placed his feet flat on the ground and leaned his elbows on his knees. "Now, boys, gather the plates and wash them in one of the buckets. The other bucket is for Tessa. I imagine the cool water will be soothing after cooking over the fire."

Tessa dropped her fan back into her knapsack. How thoughtful. Even more, how admirable to have taken on the rearing of his younger brothers.

She reached for one of the buckets, but Francis grabbed the handle. "Allow me."

"Would you bring my chair, Adam?" she asked and moved away from the campfire.

"Happy to." Adam raised the chair over his head and followed her around to the other side of the wagon.

Once they saw her settled, the boys left her alone, and she rested a moment with her eyes closed. She breathed in the air that had mercifully cooled as the setting sun turned the sky from fiery orange to crimson and then purple, all reflected in the surface of the bucket water. She dipped her kerchief into the water and sponged the dirt and grit from her face, neck, and arms, reveling in the soothing, cool droplets that trickled in between her breasts. She removed her mobcap and loosened her braid, spilling the curls around her shoulders and down her back. She tried combing her fingers through the unruly tresses, but she needed her brush.

She walked around the back of the wagon and would have called out to her father, but he had fallen sound asleep in his chair.

Stephen approached her and pressed a finger to his lips. "May I be of assistance?" he asked, keeping his voice low.

"Yes. You warned me not to get close to the wagon, but I need my brush and a bar of soap. They're in a small sealskin satchel at the back of the wagon. At least, that's where it was before the wheel broke."

She stood beside him as he opened the backboard and she caught him staring at her hair. Did he find her attractive? He certainly captured her attention.

She pointed to the satchel. "That's it, there."

He dragged it onto the backboard and waited while she rummaged through the contents and retrieved what she needed.

Stephen closed the bag and shoved it against the side of the wagon. "Anything else?"

She glanced over her shoulder at her father, whose head

had dropped onto the back of the chair. "I hate to impose, but... would you mind helping him to his pallet?"

"Certainly." He left the backboard open, approached Mr. Harris, and tapped him on his shoulder. The empty tankard fell from his lap and rolled across the ground.

Tessa's father roused with a snort and brushed his hand over his face. "Hmm? What?"

"Come with me, sir. You are tired." Stephen clasped her father underneath his armpits and lifted him from the chair.

Tessa ran ahead of them and spread covers on the ground away from the fire.

"Don't let me sleep long," Father muttered, then leaned heavily on Stephen and dropped down onto the covers. "Wanna be awake when the scout comes."

After her father turned on his side and fell asleep, Tessa returned to her chair behind the wagon and spent a while brushing the dust from her hair and re-braiding it. Refreshed, she carried the chair back to the fire and sat next to Stephen.

He balanced on the stool and pushed a hot coal back into the fire with the tip of his boot. "The boys have gone to check on the horses. They'll be back shortly."

They sat quietly a few minutes. Tessa laced her fingers together in her lap. "I don't want to pry, but what did you mean when you said your brothers had suffered?"

He shrugged. "I don't mind your questions. My father, though he was from a prominent family, had a terrible flaw. He was a gambler. And not a proficient one, with intermittent good and bad luck."

"I see." She spoke without judgment. How could she, with a drunkard for a father?

Stephen gave her a knowing look before continuing. "When I was seventeen, he had a particularly successful run of good fortune and was able to provide for my commission in the cavalry. I'd been in the army about five years when he died in a fight over cheating—someone else's—not his. Sadly, the money he left behind didn't last long, and my soldier's pay wasn't enough to keep my mother and brothers going. When my mother succumbed to a fever, everything was gone. The boys were forced to live on the charity of friends until I made my way back home."

Thoughts of Francis and Adam being mistreated saddened Tessa.

"They may seem younger than they are, for they had no real fathering. They grew up in the city without any responsibilities. And, because my mother was ill with no relatives around to help keep the boys in check, they roamed as they pleased." He frowned. "I don't think I'll ever forgive myself for not being there for them."

"Oh, no. Don't say that. I'm certain you did the best you could. You're with them now, and that is what counts. Look at them." The boys had returned to the edge of the clearing and were engaged in some sort of contest throwing rocks at trees. "I've never seen two healthier, more splendid young men."

Stephen viewed his lively brothers and chuckled. "They are quite splendid. But don't let them hear you say that."

The sound of his laughter made her smile. So did the dimple in his cheek. "What made you come to the colonies?"

"My uncle...my mother's only brother...has a horse farm in South Carolina. I contacted him, and he asked us to join him. The boys will help out on the farm, and I will train horses."

Tessa perked up. "Where in South Carolina?"

"Camden. Close to the border with North Carolina. Apparently, although it's a small settlement, it's known for horse breeding."

"Camden!" Tessa clapped her hands. "What a lovely coincidence. That's where my father and I are going, to join in business with a friend. I was hesitant about the settlement, but

Father's friend assured us that it's a thriving area large enough to support our business."

"That *is* a happy coincidence." Stephen prodded the fire with a stick and stared into the flickering flames. "Why did you and your father leave England? I would think there would be far more demands for portraits there."

Tessa looked him in the eye. "You are aware of my father's drinking."

"I am."

"It's not something easily hidden and gets worse with each passing year." She folded her hands again in her lap. "It's his way of coping with my mother's death."

His caring expression encouraged her to continue.

"He was commissioned to paint a member of the royal family in London. It was to be a present for the woman's husband's birthday. But father, due to...circumstances...was unable to finish it in time." Tessa stared up at the sky. "I offered to finish the portrait, but she had no faith in me. She made it her mission to ruin Father's reputation. She accomplished her goal well. We went months without a commission and nearly lost everything we had."

"I'm so sorry, Tessa." Stephen gazed at her with regret. "How sadly similar our stories of loss and suffering are."

"Indeed." She draped her braid across her breast.

Stephen sat forward. "What happened next?"

"Then father remembered his friend here in the colonies. They corresponded and agreed to go into business together. The gentleman is a carpenter and furniture maker who'll fashion the frames for the portraits my father and I will paint. It is a promise of a new beginning for us."

"I've often wondered..." Stephen reached inside his waistcoat and withdrew a small leather pouch. He opened the drawstring and retrieved a cameo brooch. "I've wondered if someone could copy this painting of my mother. One for each of my brothers." He held the cameo out to her.

Scars marked his long fingers. Not the hands of a drawing room dandy and ever so much more appealing.

Tessa accepted the pin from him and ran a finger across the oval surface the length of her little finger. "I've seen paintings on ivory brooches like this before, but I'm more familiar with carved cameos. Isn't it fascinating—the intricate details the artist was able to get on such a small surface?"

"Yes, amazing work. It means a great deal to me to have such a fine likeness of my mother."

He swallowed hard, and his eyes grew soft. The momentary vulnerability touched her.

Tessa studied the likeness again, looking from it to Stephen and back again. "She's stunning. I can see her in you and your brothers."

"So you could paint copies for us? For framing in Camden?" Anticipation filled his expressive face. So engaging, Tessa could not resist.

"Yes. I'd be honored."

Joy lit his eyes, accentuating their caramel-colored flecks. "You will let me know what I owe?"

"I'll let you know after I've consulted with Father. Would you allow me to hold onto it for a while? Give me time to study it and draw some drafts? I promise, I'll keep it safe."

"Of course." He handed her the pouch.

Warmed by his trust, she secured the cameo back into its cover and dropped it into her rucksack.

Francis and Adam, tired of their play, joined them.

Tessa clasped her hands together beneath her chin. "Boys, I just discovered that we will be neighbors in Camden. Isn't it grand?"

"I say." Francis plopped down with Adam on the blanket next to the fire. "That's jolly good news, Tessa."

Her father, his hair and clothing rumpled from his nap, joined them and sat in his chair.

"You are rested, Father?" His eyes were clearer. He'd slept away some of the drink.

"I'm fine." He grumbled and raked his hair back from his forehead.

Tessa pulled her art materials from her rucksack and started drawing Adam, who was rolling a red-hot pinecone in and out of the fire.

"Careful, Adam, you know how prone to accidents you are," Stephen warned.

Tessa raised an eyebrow.

"Ha! That is stating it mildly," Francis said. "Burns, scrapes, broken bones, head injuries...used to worry our mother to pieces. Once, he even tripped over his own feet and tumbled headlong down a flight of stairs. I was at the bottom and just knew he was dead. But he stood up, brushed himself off, and walked away. No damage to that thick skull."

Adam rose up onto his knees. "Are you saying my head is hard?"

Francis sat up. "If the cap fits..."

Adam shoved Francis back onto the blanket and struggled to sit on top of him, but Francis threw him off, dangerously close to the fire.

Tessa sucked in a breath.

"Boys. Enough." Stephen's gruff command ended the brawl.

Tessa flinched. She'd never want to be on the receiving end of Stephen's disapproval.

Two hours passed and then three since the wagon master had left them. Tessa sketched, then paced, then rearranged some of the food supplies Stephen had contributed and made plans for their next meal. The boys gathered wood, fed the draft horses, and practiced their sword fighting while Stephen cleaned the firearms. Father, refraining from drink, whittled pieces of wood, fashioning the ends of paint brushes. Tired of the busy work and trying to pass the time, they all eventually ended up sitting quietly a distance from the fire they kept going to keep animals at bay.

Stars punched their way through the black skies. The moon, barely visible through the trees, began its arch. Flames from the fire flickered across the surrounding tree trunks and in the limbs waving overhead. Shadows moved amidst the dense underbrush in an eerie dance. An owl hooted in the distance, running goosebumps up and down Tessa's arms.

"What is that?" Francis pointed toward the woods. "It looks like a couple of glowing marbles."

Stephen untangled his long legs and stood, pistol in hand. "Probably a wolf." He walked up and down the edge of the trail, focusing on the spot Francis had indicated. "I wouldn't worry. They don't attack humans, as a rule. They are curious, though. The wolves in India are smaller than the ones here, and their fur is gray. We often saw them peering at us from the shadows."

"His eyes are ghostly." Adam shook his shoulders. "You won't find me far from the fire."

Francis snorted. "You, of any of us, would be the one to get eaten."

They tussled a bit until Stephen threw them a scowl, then sat back down. The boys finally grew quiet and stared into the campfire.

Slumping with his legs stretched out, Tessa's father grew more morose by the minute.

On tenterhooks, Tessa kept quiet but scooted to the edge of her chair.

What was taking so long?

Father sprang to his feet. "That's it. I'm going to find out what's happening."

Stephen picked up his pistol and secured it in his belt. "Let me go. I've got my saddlehorse."

Father shook his head. "I appreciate the offer, but I must take responsibility. I'll ride one of my draft horses."

Tessa hurried to her father's side. "It's almost pitch black. Why don't you wait for them a bit longer?"

"No. This is my problem. *I* need to fix this. Not to worry, my sweet girl." He caressed her cheek, then glanced at Stephen. "You'll take care of my daughter, Mr. Griffith?"

Stephen rested a hand on the flintlock at his waist. "With my life."

The dire promise brought tears of gratitude to her eyes. She would be safe with Stephen.

The boys stood on either side of her, and Francis clasped her hand. "We'll protect her, Mr. Harris."

She squeezed Francis's hand. What dear young men.

Tessa's heart fluttered, but her mouth went dry as her father led one of the horses from the nearby field. He had bridled and mounted the horse and was preparing to leave when Stephen approached him with a lighted lantern.

"Here, sir." Stephen handed him the light. "This will help until the moon grows a bit brighter."

As her father rode up the trail and darkness engulfed him, Tessa whispered, "Dear Lord, please keep him safe. He's all I have in this world."

CHAPTER 3

*N*ot long after her father left, Stephen kept the fire going while Tessa paced up and down the trail from the campfire to the outer reaches of its flames.

"Something is wrong. I feel it," she said, standing in the middle of the trail and wringing her hands.

Stephen joined her. "I agree."

Far too much time had passed since the wagon master promised to send help. The same gut instincts that had roused his alarm before the devastating Battle of Mumbai made the hair on the back of his neck tingle. He masked his apprehension, even though Tessa had voiced her anxiety.

Tessa balled her fists by her sides. "I'm not sure how much longer I can bear waiting here. Doing nothing. I cannot imagine what could have happened to Father...and the others."

Tessa's face had paled, and worry filled her eyes. Stephen needed to take charge and remain positive.

"I wanted to go see for myself but thought better of it. Whatever we do, we must stay together." Stephen pressed his fists onto his hips. "Francis. Adam. Come join us," he called out.

The boys, who had been practicing with mock swords, threw down their sticks and came to Stephen's side.

"Tessa and I are concerned about Mr. Harris and also why we haven't heard from the rest of the train. We're trying to decide whether to stay here until morning or to go now and see what's happened. Tessa and I want to go straight away. What say you?"

Francis, his earnest expression now turned serious, spoke first. "I'm for finding out sooner rather than later."

Adam held up his hand as if voting. "Me too."

"Right, then. I'm thinking, based on what Mr. Washburn said, the train bedded down for the night about ten to fifteen miles up the trail...an hour or more away. Tessa will ride with me on Knight, and you can double up on one of the draft horses. Gather a lantern, a flint box, and a couple of canteens. Make sure the canteens are full. Then saddle Knight and bring him and one of the horses."

"Should I bring my medicine kit?" Tessa asked as they walked back to the campfire.

"No. We need to travel light. The evening is cool, though, so wear something to cover your arms." He pointed to a chair. "Wait there and let us take care of things."

She stared at him a moment.

He stretched his arms out toward her. "Forgive me. I should have said *please*. But I'm used to giving orders. It's my way."

Tessa sat in her chair near the campfire. "I understand. And I'm not complaining. For the first time in a long while, I am to wait and rely on someone else with more experience and ability than myself. You cannot imagine the relief I'm feeling."

Stephen nodded and offered her a small smile. He had promised her father he would guard her with his life, and he intended to keep that promise. But in doing so, he needed to protect her, not overpower her.

Stephen and his brothers made quick work of dousing the

fire, gathering food and water, and managing the horses. When he spanned Tessa's waist with his hands and lifted her onto his horse, he had to maneuver around the sword strapped around his waist and the pistol stuffed into his belt. The boys mounted their horse without their usual tussle over who should take the reins.

Stephen slid his foot into the stirrup and swept up into the saddle behind Tessa. He stretched his arms around her to secure the reins. He pressed her slender body against his chest and breathed in the slight aroma of roses on her skin.

A full moon positioned straight overhead reflected off the ruts in the sandy trail, transforming it into a white satin ribbon. They began at a canter but soon slowed down to spare the draft horse that was not accustomed to speed.

They had ridden for close to an hour when Francis coughed. "Ugh. What's that smell?"

Stephen had been in enough battles to know exactly what it was—burning flesh.

Something terrible awaited them around the bend.

He slid off his horse and helped a trembling Tessa dismount. She landed with her feet on the ground and her face nestled in his chest. He longed to hold her...to prepare her for what might await them.

"Tessa, you should remain here while we reconnoiter." He led her to a fallen tree trunk at the edge of the trail and tied Knight to a branch. "Please...please, Tessa. Promise me you will not follow us."

She threw her shawl over her shoulders and wrapped it tightly around her body. "I promise, but you must assure me in return. You will let me know something soon about my father."

Francis tethered the draft horse next to Knight, lit a lantern from a flint box, and placed it at Tessa's feet. "We'll come and get you as soon as we can."

Stephen walked away with his brothers, and as they neared

a bend in the road, the muscles across his neck and shoulders quivered. His fighting instincts had come alive long before he smelled burning flesh.

What lay ahead? What was he exposing his brothers to?

He looked over his shoulder at Tessa. What of her father?

CHAPTER 4

*T*hey rounded the bend and beheld the destroyed campsite.

Bodies—their arms, legs, and torsos splayed at odd angles —were strewn everywhere. Most, from what Stephen could tell, had been mortally wounded by arrows. The moon, an eerie beacon, cast ghastly shadows over the faces revealing their horror, pain, and surprise.

Adam gasped and covered his nose and mouth with his hand. Francis stood ramrod stiff. Stephen stopped breathing until his lungs ached.

It was the stuff of nightmares. Something that would forever mark the day his brothers left behind their boyhoods.

Adam doubled over and vomited. Francis, his eyes swimming in tears, clasped his younger brother across his shoulders.

"Steady on." Stephen barely croaked the words.

Scouring the grounds and a nearby wagon, finding no lanterns intact, he quickly gathered branches, cloths, and lantern oil and fashioned torches that he lit and handed to the boys. He held his torch overhead and perused the massacre.

Canvases had been torn from wagon beds, some of which

still smoldered. Much of the wagon contents, what had not been carried away, had been dragged into the center of the campsite and thrown onto a pile, creating a huge bonfire. The charred skeleton of one pour soul lay on the pinnacle, tossed there by his murderers.

Stephen swallowed against the bile that collected in the back of his throat. "We must see if anyone survived."

It would be a miracle.

Stephen raised his torch higher. "Check for horses and live-stock, too, though I'm certain the Indians made away with them all."

He searched underneath the wagons as well as the perimeter of the camp in the hope that someone may have taken shelter there but found no one. The boys, who had pulled their shirts up over their noses, tiptoed around the bodies and leaned down attempting to detect any life. The bodies of Mr. Washburn and the scout, both of whom had been bludgeoned with a hatchet, had fallen close together near the bonfire ashes. With his backbone as rigid as steel, Stephen moved from one corpse to the next—seventeen victims, all adults, as there had been no children with the train. A small mercy.

Would they have killed children? He shuddered at the thought.

In the short time they had spent together, Stephen had become acquainted with many of the travelers. The young newlywed couple now lay entwined near their wagon, having shared their last breaths together. One man had thrown his body over his wife's in a futile attempt to shield her. The wagoners had come from many different places and back-grounds, but they had all shared something in common—the promise of a new and better life.

What a sad, dreadful ending to those promises.

"Stephen." Francis's voice startled him. "We found Mr. Harris." He pointed to the edge of the clearing. "Over there."

Stephen followed his brothers to the place where Mr. Harris had fallen onto his side. An arrow had pierced his chest and had shot straight through his ribcage and out his back.

Eighteen victims.

Stephen removed his sword and laid it on the ground. He knelt and broke off the tip of the arrow, pulled the shaft from Mr. Harris's body, and rolled him over onto his back.

"Bring me that blanket there on the ground, please, Adam. We'll cover his wound so Tessa doesn't have to witness it."

Francis squatted next to Stephen. "Should we tell Tessa now? We told her we would let her know something as soon as possible."

Stephen gritted his teeth. "I'll go. You and Adam see if you can find shovels. We must bury these people soon before animals discover their scent. Start...there." He indicated a plot of ground near the opening of the circled wagons. "We'll dig one mass grave."

The boys set about to follow his instructions, their eyes wide in their pale faces, their jaws clenched.

As Stephen left the clearing, he lifted up a fervent prayer asking for guidance and for the most compassionate words to share with Tessa. He prayed his brothers would not be scarred by the terrible experience.

When he reached Tessa, he stopped to watch her. Huddled on a log, wrapped in an overlarge shawl, she seemed even smaller than usual. She had draped her braid over her shoulder, and the lantern light cast a glow on the curls that feathered around her face. Her ever-present rucksack lay at her feet. The moment she spotted him, she jumped up and ran to him.

"Let's sit back down." Stephen clasped her by her elbow and sat with her on the log.

"I can tell by your face—the news isn't good." She bit down on her bottom lip.

Stephen filled his lungs with air and blew it out slowly. "It could not be worse. The wagon train was attacked by Indians, and there is not one survivor."

Tessa's face crumpled. "So...my father?"

Stephen's shoulders sagged. He could do nothing to soften the blow. "Your father was among them."

Tessa covered her face with her hands and cried, bone-shaking, shuddering sobs that tore at Stephen's heart. He scooted closer to her and draped his arm across her back. Rocking back and forth, he cradled her until her normal breathing returned.

"How did he die? Did he suffer? Can I see him?" She spoke the questions without taking a breath, her eyes so full of pain he could barely meet them.

"He was felled by an arrow, and, no, I don't think he suffered. You could see him now, but I'd like to clear some space for you. There are things I do not wish for you to see."

She gripped the open edges of his shirt. "I would like to come now, if I may. It's so very lonely out here." She took a fleeting look across the trail at the woods. "Will the Indians come back?"

She shook with fright, and he yearned to sweep her up into his arms.

"As far as I can determine by their tracks, they moved away going east." He picked up the lantern and offered his other arm for support. "Come. And know that I'm right here with you."

They moved along silently until Stephen felt compelled to speak again. "My brothers and I are digging one grave. It makes more sense that way."

"I understand." Tessa's jaw muscles quivered.

"We could prepare a separate one for your father—"

"No. The three of you will be exhausted enough. I think my

father would be...would be honored to share a resting place with the others."

They reached the clearing, and Stephen moved in front of her to block her view of the carnage. "Your father is there, near the edge of the campsite."

Slowly, hesitantly placing one foot in front of the other, Tessa crept toward her father's body. One of Stephen's brothers had covered him with a blanket, tucking it underneath his chin.

"He looks as though he's sleeping," she whispered.

She knelt beside him and reached under the cover to hold his hand. She stroked his long fingers. "His beautiful hands. They created some of the most inspiring art I have ever known. They held my hands when I was a child, teaching me, guiding me."

She gently tucked his hand beneath the cover, and with tears spilling down her cheeks, she looked up at Stephen. "He's finally happy. He's with our Lord and with the love of his life."

Stephen cleared his throat, struggled to speak, and cleared his throat again. "I hate to leave you, Tessa, but we must lay these poor people to rest soon. Will you be all right?"

She placed her hand on her father's leg. "You do what needs to be done. I'll keep vigil here until it's time."

Stephen walked away but stopped and looked over his shoulder. Tessa wept softly beside her father's body, her shoulders drooped, her head bowed.

He would make it his mission to find something to ease her pain.

CHAPTER 5

*P*ink-tipped fingers of dawn had pulled back the curtain of night when Stephen spread the last shovel of soil over the grave. Sweat rolled down his chest and arms, carving rivulets through the dirt-encrusted skin. Francis and Adam positioned themselves between him and Tessa, their knees trembling with exhaustion, their grimy, tear-stained faces white from the trauma.

Stephen clasped his hands together in front of him and bowed his head. "Heavenly Father, it is so very difficult to find the words." He paused. "Please welcome the souls of our brothers and sisters so that they may rejoice in You and with Your saints forever."

He opened his eyes and draped his arm across Adam's shoulder. "I am reminded of our mother's favorite hymn and how the words gave her comfort." He recited the first stanza aloud.

> Time, like an ever-rolling stream,
> Bears all its sons away;
> They fly forgotten, as a dream

Dies at the opening day.

Adam and Francis spoke the words of the last chorus with him, eliciting a whimper from Tessa.

> O God, our help in ages past,
> Our hope for years to come,
> Be thou our guard while troubles last,
> And our eternal home."

She kissed Adam's cheek and did the same to Francis. "Thank you, boys. You have behaved quite wonderfully, and I shall never forget it."

Stephen pulled a gold band from his pocket and handed it to her. "I thought you might want this."

"Father's ring." Her lips quivered. "Thank you. Thank you for your courage and for what you have done here."

They walked away from the clearing and gathered on the trail.

Stephen stretched his arms rigidly by his sides. "We've plenty of decisions to make. We need to get as far away from here and as soon as possible. But first, the boys and I must clean up."

Tessa grimaced at their filthy, blood-stained garments.

Stephen held up a bar of soap. "I found this. We passed a creek just down the road. Tessa, do you want to ride or walk?"

"I'll walk."

Once again, Stephen stuffed the pistol into his belt and carried his sword. "Francis, you lead the horses. Adam, load that canvas bag onto the draft horse."

When they reached a path leading to the creek, they tethered the horses near a patch of grass and removed Knight's saddle. At the top of the bank, Tessa sat on the moss-covered ground and leaned back against the trunk of an oak tree.

Stephen placed his pistol and sword beside her and joined the boys, pulling off their boots and jumping straight into the waist-high water. They soon lathered the soap all over their clothing and in their hair and plunged deep into the water to rinse.

Stephen scrubbed and scrubbed until his skin grew raw. He watched the boys closely. Even though the soap washed away the scent of death, nothing could ever erase the dark memories that must be lurking in their minds.

Tessa, sitting with her back against the tree trunk, gazed off into the woods in a daze. She had placed her sketchbook across her lap, but her pencil remained dormant.

She had backbone. Her father's death had been a blow, but she was a survivor. Even so, she and his brothers required attention. Having experienced the equivalent to battle trauma, they all needed to start building memories...good ones...to allay the painful, nightmarish ones.

During the dreadful night, he had kept his mind occupied considering his next steps. During the past two days they had ventured into Virginia, having covered only a third of the journey to Camden. They could turn back and try to find another wagon train to join. But he did not want to go backward, only forward.

What of Tessa?

She walked to the edge of the creek, and holding her petticoats up around her knees, she waded barefoot in the shallows, picking her way carefully among the pebbles. She doused her kerchief into the water and sponged it down her arms and wrapped it around her neck. She bent down and picked up a feather that she slipped into her under-pocket, her movements graceful. Appealing. She returned to the oak tree, but with her head bowed and shoulders drooping, she reminded him of a forlorn sunflower battered by a storm.

Even if they repaired her wagon, how could she manage?

She was a single woman, alone in the wilderness, vulnerable. He bore no obligation to her. They barely knew one another. She needed help, but if he offered that help, it would be a huge responsibility. He already had his brothers to care for. Mentally and physically exhausted, he dipped down into the water once more and then climbed up the bank.

"I needed that," he said, stretching out on the moss beside Tessa.

She didn't respond but concentrated on putting her sketchbook and pencil into her rucksack.

"Tessa, I'm curious. Do you collect feathers?"

Seemingly caught off guard, Tessa lifted an eyebrow.

Stephen stretched his arms over his head and yawned. "I saw you pick one up and save it in your pocket."

She retrieved the feather from her under-pocket and put it into her rucksack. "I use them as brushes sometimes, especially if I'm painting a young child. They help me to create fine curls of hair."

Stephen lay down and threw his arm over his eyes. "I shall be on the lookout for more feathers, then."

The boys ran up the bank and lay on the other side of Tessa. They remained quiet, subdued, and soon fell sound asleep. The last thing Stephen saw before he succumbed to sleep was Adam stretching out his arm and curling his fingers into Tessa's hand.

His brothers were fond of Tessa. So was he. He had many decisions to make.

Lord, guide me, please.

CHAPTER 6

wo hours later, after the men indulged in their much-needed nap, Tessa spent time in prayer while Stephen took the boys aside. Was he reassuring them? Listening to their reactions? What could she do to help them return to normal after they lived through such a horrible experience? How could she help anyone when she was barely coping?

Finally, they set out for their abandoned wagons. Along the way, the boys continued to complain.

"I'm so hungry, I might faint," Adam whined.

"Faint? Huh. I'm about ready to eat this horse," Francis countered. "How much longer before we get there?"

"That's enough." Stephen's chest rumbled against Tessa's back as they rode together on Knight.

She shared his aggravation with his brothers' constant grumbling, but their banter was a welcome sign that their spirits had rallied.

Stephen's strong, tanned arms kept her secure in the saddle. Though his capable hands held Knight's reins, he had not used those reins, but guided with his knees and feet. Master and mount moved as one. She enjoyed the feel of him and the warmth of his breath against her neck. As she studied the scars on his fingers, a vision of her father's hands entered her mind, and she sucked in a breath.

"Is something amiss, Tessa?" Stephen pulled the reins and halted.

"My father..." Her body shook. "What am I to do without him?"

He dismounted and helped her down. "Boys, we're stopping for a few minutes. You stay right here and watch the horses."

Adam groaned. "But what about food?"

Stephen's frown and raised eyebrow curtailed any more protests.

He and Tessa moved a distance away from his brothers. "I know you grieve. And this isn't the most appropriate time to be making important decisions. But you're already wondering what you will do. Are you not?"

She pressed her fingers against her temples. "I prayed this morning that God would give me strength and show me the way. Somewhere among my father's belongings is the name of the man we were to meet in Camden, but I don't know him. Will he still want to work with me? Without my father? I'm alone now. I have no one left on this earth. And that stuns me."

"Don't worry, Tessa. The boys and I decided that we don't want to go back to Philadelphia and possibly join another train. We want to travel on to South Carolina. Is that something you'd consider? Because..." He hesitated. "If you do, we'd like to invite you to come along with us."

The sincerity in his golden-brown eyes comforted her.

"Truly?" Her voice cracked with emotion. "I wouldn't be a burden?"

"Not at all." He shrugged. "The boys like you. I like you. And..." He grinned. "You make a fine quartermaster."

Gratitude and relief overwhelmed her, and she could not

hold back the tears that trickled down her cheeks. "If you're sure. I'd like very much to join you."

"I was hoping you'd say that. Consider this—instead of repairing your wagon, it would be best if we combine our wagons. Put your things in ours. To be honest, we hardly have any possessions, anyway. One wagon would be easier to defend. And we could sell your horses. Use the money for supplies."

He continued to speak, but Tessa did not hear much after he said he hoped she would accompany them. Despite his denial, she *would* be an extra responsibility for him. She welcomed his kindness and generosity so much, she struggled against the impulse to throw her arms around his neck.

When the boys heard their decision, they cheered but spoke again about eating the hind end of a Billy goat. Spurred by that, their little band of travelers continued on until mid-afternoon when they reached the wagons.

Stephen dismounted and took Tessa by the waist to help her down, and her stomach grumbled so loud, he chuckled. "Someone else is mighty hungry."

She enjoyed the dimple his smile made in his cheek and resisted pushing back the tendril of hair that had dropped onto his forehead. "It will have to be corncakes and bacon again."

"I'll build a fire, and the boys will water the horses and then help you with whatever you need."

He stepped away, and Tessa missed the warmth of his hands on her waist.

"'Lo the camp," a voice called out from the forest ahead.

Stephen pulled the pistol from his belt, shoved Tessa behind him, and yelled to the boys, "To me!"

Francis and Adam, who had been gathering wood for the fire, came running. They all huddled together as two men approached the camp on horseback, each leading a heavily laden mule.

"We don't mean you no harm," the first man said, holding

his hands in the air. "I'm Jefferson, and this is Reynolds. Trappers taking our hides to the trading post a ways down the trail."

They stopped their horses close by and dismounted, wafting the smell of tobacco and a thousand campfires around them. Their fringed breeches and jackets were streaked with animal fat, bloodstains, and dirt.

Jefferson, the taller of the two, reached out his hand to Stephen, who shook it after switching the pistol to his other hand. Reynolds, a short, stocky man, followed suit.

"I'm Stephen Griffith, and this is Miss Harris. These are my brothers, Francis and Adam."

The two men tipped their hats. Tessa stepped from behind Stephen and curtsied. The boys bowed.

Jefferson grinned, accentuating the deep furrows at the corners of his tobacco-colored eyes. "The boys have manners. That's a good sign."

"What happened here?" Jefferson asked and then walked away to inspect the broken wheel. "And what are you doing out here with only two wagons? Nobody comes this way much except wagon trains. It's a dangerous section of the trail. Most of the locals around these parts move by river."

Francis and Adam went back to gathering the cookware and piling up firewood. Eager to speed up the preparation of their meal, they built a campfire in the middle of the trail, and around it they placed two chairs, a stool, and a blanket.

"We were part of a train that left out of Philadelphia," Stephen answered, still resting his arm against the pistol he had returned to his belt. "When the Harrises' wagon wheel broke, my brothers and I stayed behind with them while the rest of the train moved up the trail and made camp about an hour away. They were attacked by Indians. It was a massacre. No survivors."

Jefferson scowled and drew his eyebrows up while glancing at Reynolds. "You sure it was Indians?"

"They died from arrow wounds." Tessa pressed a hand to her stomach. "Including my father."

The trappers pulled off their hats and spoke in unison. "So sorry for your loss."

Stephen pressed a fist to his hip. "We gave them a Christian burial. Just got back from doing so, in fact. But isn't there some authority I can report to about what happened?"

"Ha!" Jefferson pursed his bottom lip. "No law out here. There's a fort about three days' ride. But they won't help. The only reason the British government gave land to settlers is to provide a buffer between the coast and the Indians. It's up to the settlers to defend themselves."

Tessa moved away to stand by Adam, who sat on the blanket positioning the frying pan closer to the fire. "Excuse me, gentlemen, but the boys are famished, and I must get supper started. You're welcome to join us, though it's just corn-cakes and bacon."

Jefferson strode over to one of the mules and pulled a bundle out from under a canvas. "Let me see what we can do about that." He joined Tessa by the fire and sat in one of the chairs. "If you don't mind, I'll do the honors this evening. You rest."

Stephen and Reynolds came to stand at the edge of the blanket. Making a big show, Jefferson reached into a large leather sack. Creating a fanfare like a magician, he drew out an onion, a bundle of wild scallions, a bulb of garlic, a sack of flour, and pieces of red meat. The men sighed with pleasure and expressed their anticipation. While strips of bacon simmered, rendering grease, Jefferson crushed a pod of garlic and swirled it around in the pan.

"What is that meat?" Tessa asked.

"Bear. Nice black mountain bear that fed on berries, grasses, and roots. It makes their meat much sweeter." He cut the strips into bite-sized pieces and dusted them with flour.

"This is the secret. Making sure each piece gets soaked in the seasoning."

He pulled the cork top from a clay pot, dumped cooked beans into a pan, and laid pieces of scallion on top.

Tessa, unwilling to rest and give her mind time to think about her father, made corncakes and stacked them onto a platter. Despite her growling stomach, she grew queasier with each passing moment.

Stephen and his brothers sat on the blanket, watching Reynolds's every move. Adam's eyes grew as big around as one of her artist pallets. Tessa glanced from him to Francis and then to Stephen. The expressions of rapture on their faces made her smile.

When all was ready and a blessing said, the men pounced on the food as if they had not eaten in weeks. Though she served herself a plate, Tessa refrained from eating as a picture of her father's favorite mincemeat pie came to mind. She would never be able to cook it for him again.

"Oh, my," Adam said, his cheeks bulging.

"Don't talk with your mouth full," Stephen admonished, his own mouth crammed with food.

"Well..." Jefferson sopped the last of the gravy with a piece of corncake. "I feel as if I've dined with pharaoh's locusts."

Stephen took a swallow of water from his canteen. "You're not eating, Tessa?"

Without warning, a flood of tears rolled down her face. She stood up and fled to the other side of her wagon. Holding onto the wheel, she grabbed her mobcap and pressed it to her mouth to muffle her sobs.

A pair of hands rested on her shoulders. Stephen gently turned her around and into his arms. She dropped her mobcap, gripped the sides of his waistcoat, and pressed her face into his chest. Painful sobs wracked her body, and Stephen's embrace was the only thing keeping her from falling. When her tears abated, she stepped back, and he wiped her face with his kerchief.

"I am sorry." Her words came weak and hoarse.

He picked up her mobcap. "You have nothing to apologize for, Tessa. I feel I should apologize as I don't seem to have the right words to say. What can I do to help?"

Her lips trembled as she attempted to smile. "You already have."

He arranged her mobcap on her head and tucked in the loose tendrils on either side of her face. The caring gesture almost undid Tessa, and she longed for him to hold her once more.

She pressed her hands to her cheeks and sucked in a deep breath.

"Better now?" He returned his handkerchief into his waistcoat pocket.

"Better."

He offered his elbow, and she curled her arm around it. When they returned to the others, Stephen held her chair for her to sit. Jefferson awaited her with a cup of water, and the boys quietly washed and dried the dishes. Reynolds played a soothing tune on his harmonica.

Their kindness and care flowed across her tattered heart as a healing balm. God walked with her through her valley. His love would sustain her through whatever lay ahead.

CHAPTER 7

The following morning, they awoke at sunrise to what promised to be a day of sunshine, but also unrelenting heat. After breakfast, Stephen gathered with the men next to the disabled wagon to form a plan. They each brought tools they had on hand and lay them beside the broken wheel.

Reynolds kicked the wheel. "We could try dragging it down the trail."

"Nope." Jefferson squinted ahead. "This part of the trail is too narrow. There's not a clearing to dump it in for over a mile. It would be too hard on the horses, anyway."

Stephen considered the wreckage and shrugged. "We could take it apart and carry the pieces into the forest."

"There you have it." Jefferson snapped his fingers. "One thing I'd advise is keep one of the wheels. Lash it underneath the other wagon in case of future problems."

"Good thought." Stephen added a hammer to the pile of tools. "Let's get started moving the cargo out of this one."

It took about an hour to transfer almost everything from Tessa's wagon. While Stephen and Francis balanced on the backboard, Tessa sorted through a polished oak chest containing her father's belongings.

"Has his entire life truly dwindled to fit into this one small chest?" She closed the latch. "No. I refuse to think that. He left behind an incredible legacy—beautiful creations, portraits telling the stories of hundreds of people revealed through their expressions he had captured on canvas. I couldn't be more proud."

"Fine sentiments, Tessa," Francis said and then looked away. "Not everyone's father can be remembered so well."

At his brother's sad statement, Stephen's heart lurched.

Tessa rubbed her fingers across the letters of her father's name engraved on the metal plate fastened to the top of the trunk. "Stephen told me something of your father, Francis. He made mistakes. We all do. Do not dwell on bad memories, but try to recall some of the good times you had with your father."

Francis ducked his head. "I'll try, Tessa."

Her father's trunk was the last thing to go, and as she handed it to Francis, she wiped the tears from her face and scanned the canvas ceiling. "It looks so much larger in here now that it's empty."

Stooped over, she walked to the backboard where Stephen beckoned with open arms.

"All will be well," he whispered and swung her down.

With her hands on his shoulders, she sighed. "I want so much to believe you."

His hands encompassed her tiny waist. How delicate she was. By agreeing to travel with him, she had placed herself under his protection. Her body might be petite, but the responsibility of keeping her safe would be massive. Was he up to the task? He was, and the more he learned of her, the more he wanted it.

They remained thus for a few moments, then parted to

make way for the others who approached the wagon holding hammers and axes.

The dismantling of Tessa's wagon took the men a couple of hours. By that time, everyone was dirty, sweaty, and hot, not only from the strenuous work, but because the air sweltered.

Jefferson swabbed his clammy forehead with a handkerchief. "Phew! Glad that's over. It's so hot, I could fry an egg on your bald head, Reynolds."

Reynolds cackled and rubbed his hand across his head. He waggled his wiry gray eyebrows, sending Adam and Francis into laughter.

Jefferson moved toward his mule. "Miss Harris, you might want to spread some bear grease on your nose and arms. I've got some in my pack, if you'd like."

She wrinkled her nose. "No, thank you. That's very kind, but I've smelled that concoction, and I think I'd rather tolerate the sunshine."

Stephen tried not to stare at her nose and arms and neck, which were all quite pink. She ran her fingers across the definite sunburn line that colored the skin around the edge of her tucker.

Stephen frowned. "At least wear your hat, Tessa."

She knitted her brows and jerked down on the edges of her mobcap. "Yes, Stephen."

Was she irritated with him? He *was* ordering her around again.

Jefferson glanced back and forth between them. "I'm headed for the creek. Gonna take this bucket and douse my head with some of that cold water coming down from the mountains."

Tessa plopped on her straw hat and tied the ribbons underneath the back of her hair. "Let's all go."

They gathered buckets, canteens, blankets, and drying cloths and headed across the field where the horses and mules foraged the grass. They arrived at the creek, and the boys removed their shoes and stockings, rolled up their pants, and waded barefoot in the knee-deep water, occasionally splashing each other until their clothes were soaked. Tessa tiptoed barefooted across rocks that lined the creek's edge. Reynolds leaned his musket up against a tree and walked out to the middle of the creek. He lay down on his back, filled his mouth with water, and squirted it out in a stream.

"You look like the fountain in our town square," Adam shouted.

Francis doubled over laughing. "Good one, Adam."

Once they cooled off, Stephen and Jefferson climbed up the bank and sat next to the blankets and the pistol Stephen kept close by.

Jefferson faced Stephen. "I'm about to say something. I mean no disrespect, but you may not like it."

Stephen cocked his head. "Go on."

"You say you're traveling on to South Carolina?"

Stephen nodded.

"That's about three or four weeks, barring any setbacks."

"About."

"Did it occur to you the position you will be putting Tessa in? An unmarried woman traveling alone with a single man?"

Stephen's back stiffened. "We would not...I would never take advantage of her. If that's what you're implying."

"You're a gentleman and Tessa's a fine, gentle lady. Good people. Me, I wouldn't think of anything unfitting happening between you, but others may and many likely will."

Stephen resented the way the conversation was going. "My brothers are with us."

"No one would consider them proper chaperones." Jefferson held out his hands. "Think, man. Right now, only Reynolds and I know your situation. But you'll pass by forts, trading posts, and settlements. Mean spirits and sharp tongues can do a passel of harm. Her reputation would be in tatters, and even though we're in the wilderness, something like that follows a person."

Stephen's stomach knotted. Where was Reynolds going with this conversation? He shrugged. "What would you have me do? I promised her we'd travel together to Camden. She's counting on it."

Jefferson moved his hands to his lap and tapped his pudgy, scarred fingers together, forming a cathedral. "Have you thought of marriage?"

Stephen would not have been more surprised if Jefferson had hit him over the head with his musket. "What? We hardly know each other."

"And yet, you've shared and survived something terrible together. It's a bond many couples don't have."

Tessa splashed the water with her dainty toes, and Stephen swallowed hard.

Jefferson untangled wet pieces of fringe down the side of his pants. "I see the way you're looking at her now. You both have some feelings for each other. I've witnessed it."

Stephen shook his head. "I-I'm at a loss."

"There's a fort, Fort Hampton, three days up the trail. See how the both of you are met. If it's not good, then get with the commandant. He can marry you." Jefferson stood, groaning at the popping of his stiff joints. "I'm saying this as a friend. I don't like to meddle in other people's business, but I like that little lady, and I wouldn't want nothing to ever cause her pain." He held out his hand.

Stephen shook Jefferson's hand and walked away with plenty to think about.

~

*A*fter an evening of Jefferson's storytelling and Reynolds playing tunes on his harmonica, everyone bedded down early—the men and boys on bedrolls and Tessa in Stephen's wagon.

Tessa had almost fallen asleep when she caught the sound of a pitiful cry. She sat up and heard it again. She threw her shawl over her shift and tried to climb over the back of the wagon, searching for the step with her toes.

When a pair of strong arms enfolded her and lifted her to the ground, she nearly shrieked. She whirled around and found her face planted in Stephen's bare chest.

She stepped back, and he lowered his arms. The bright moonlight splayed across his muscular shoulders. Try as she might, she could not keep her eyes from following the path of his chest hairs that disappeared underneath the waistline of his breeches. Unfamiliar feelings, at once pleasant and frightening, stirred her body.

"All is well, Tessa. It's Adam. He had a nightmare." He looked back over his shoulder. "I'm not surprised, after what he and Francis endured."

His hair flowed loosely about his neck. What would it feel like to run her fingers through it?

Distracted, she searched for words. "Should I go to him?"

"That's kind, but I think not. We'll see to him."

He leaned into her, reaching around to lower the back-board, and Tessa's heart tripped from the feel of him against her skin. He swept her up and lifted her onto the wagon bed. She yearned to remain in his wonderfully secure embrace a while longer.

"Get some rest," he said gruffly. "We've much to do tomorrow."

She crawled back onto the covers, rose up on her elbow, and watched him walk away to the campfire. How could she go back to sleep? Which had disturbed her most, Adam's cry or Stephen's embrace?

~

*B*efore dropping down onto his pallet, Stephen patted Adam on his shoulder. "Can you go back to sleep?"

Adam yawned. "I think so. I'm sorry to have disturbed everyone."

"There's nothing to be sorry about. Promise me, though, that you will share any worries you have with me. We...all of us have been through much. I am here for you. I love you, my brother."

"Thank you. I don't believe I've ever said it, but I love you too." Adam rolled away onto his side.

Using his hands as a pillow, Stephen lay on his back and gazed up at the stars. He rubbed one of his hands across his chest where Tessa's lips had touched his skin.

How warm and soft she felt in his arms. She was lovely. And brave. She heard a scream and hurried to help. What would marriage be like between them? She was young with a promising life ahead of her. Would she settle for a marriage of convenience based on friendship? And...attraction.

CHAPTER 8

*W*atching Jefferson and Reynolds ride away into the forest filled Tessa with sadness. They had been good for Adam and Francis. Especially Adam, who became the proud recipient of Jefferson's knife that he now wore strapped around his waist. After a few lessons, Reynolds had given Francis a harmonica. Adam laughed at the squeaking, squealing noises his brother created, sounds that made Tessa flinch.

It amazed her how quickly the two gruff, yet cordial and generous, men had become dear to her. They seemed truly humbled by the sketches she gifted them—one a portrait of Reynolds that featured his jolly countenance, and the other that captured Jefferson's honest intelligence.

Will I ever see them again? God, please, grant them traveling mercies.

Tessa waited while Stephen harnessed the four draft horses to the wagon. Jefferson and Reynolds had paid for the three horses left from Tessa's wagon, assured that they would get a fair price at the trading post they patronized.

When all was ready, the boys helped Tessa up onto the

wagon seat and settled on either side of her. Stephen rode beside them on Knight.

"Wagons, ho!" Francis shouted, mimicking their former wagon master's rally.

Tessa recalled the first time she heard that cry and the high hopes it awakened. How sad that tragedy had dwindled their train to only one wagon. She tightened the steamers of her hat.

The horses dug their hooves into the sand, and the wheels rolled forward, popping and cracking, marking the end of her father's dream and the beginning of a new set of promises.

By late morning as they neared the clearing where the Indian attack occurred, Tessa's stomach churned.

"Stephen, can we stop a moment?" she called out to him. "I don't need to get down. I need only to sit a few minutes and gather my thoughts."

"Certainly. I'll ride up ahead. Do you have this, boys?"

Adam nodded and reached for Tessa's hand.

Tessa's grief permeated every part of her. Not wanting to upset the boys, she struggled against the urge to cry.

Adam squeezed her hand. "Go ahead and cry. Francis and I both cried massive tears when we lost our mother. We know how you feel."

Tessa sucked in a deep breath and managed to squeak out the words, "Thank you, dear ones."

Stephen returned and positioned Knight close to the wagon. "If you care to visit your father's gravesite, Tessa, we can stay there as long as you want. There are some wildflowers nearby. It's up to you."

"I'd like to."

When they reached the site of the attack, Stephen showed Tessa the patch of wildflowers and held out his hat to hold the blossoms she gathered. The four of them stood quietly next to the grave while she scattered the flowers across the ground that already showed signs of returning to nature.

Did Stephen and the boys also relive that night? How long would it take each of them to put those memories to rest? She avoided the remnants of the wagon train, which eventually would be overgrown with vines and underbrush. Would future travelers come upon the site and wonder what had happened?

It was too sad to think about.

A strange *clunk, clunk, clunk* carried from the woods. "Did you hear that?"

Stephen, Francis, and Adam had all swung around toward the sound.

"Yes," Adam exclaimed. "There it is again."

The limbs of a nearby bush rustled, and Tessa hastened to Stephen's side. Moments later, a goat stuck its head through the branches and lumbered out onto the sand.

"Would you look at that?" Adam approached the docile animal and grasped the tattered rope tied around its neck.

"It must have been one of the herd that belonged to the Kerns," said Francis, scratching the goat's ears.

Tessa dropped to her knees and flung her arms around its neck. "You poor thing."

Stephen pressed a fist into his hip. "Wait. Wait."

She and the boys challenged him with similar questioning expressions.

"No. We can't keep her."

When they maintained the same expressions, he shook his head. "Is there one among us who even knows how to care for a goat? Look at her udder. It's full. Do you know how to milk her? Besides, she'll slow us down."

"It can't be that difficult to care for a goat, Stephen. Would you really leave her out here to face heaven knows what?" Tessa tightened her grip and pleaded her case with her eyes.

She knew the moment he gave in and rewarded him with a huge smile. He rolled his eyes and mounted Knight.

"I say." Francis swept his arm across the goat's back. "This is jolly good."

"What shall we name her?" asked Adam, who knelt beside Tessa. "You do the honors, Tessa."

She ruffled the goat's ears. "I've always liked the name Sally."

"Sally, it is." Francis tweaked the goat's ears.

After Adam secured the goat to the wagon with a new rope, he, Tessa, and Francis climbed aboard. When the wagon started to move, she leaned out to check on Sally, who waddled along chewing contentedly on a lump of weeds.

Something had survived after all.

She bade her father a last goodbye and gave her attention to the road ahead.

The rest of the morning, travel went smoothly. When she needed to stretch her legs, they stopped long enough for her to get down.

Adam scurried down from the wagon. "May I walk with you, Tessa?"

"I would love that. There's an old saying one of my Irish friends shared with me, 'Two people shorten the road.'"

They had walked about a half mile when Adam slowed his pace. "Tessa, when did you know that you wanted to be an artist?"

"The urge to draw and paint has always been with me. When I was a young girl, my father allowed me to explore his studio. I would run the brushes up and down my arms." She rubbed her arm and gave a faint smile. "I loved the smells, even the linseed oil and turpentine. I found it fascinating to squish the tubes of paint that were stored in animal bladders."

Adam stopped in his tracks. "Animal bladders! Surely not."

She chuckled. "Surely, yes. Bladders keep oil paints fresh. My father would poke them with a sharpened piece of bone or a needle to get the paint out."

Adam snorted. "I never would have connected animal bladders and bones with art."

"Has something...a profession...caught your interest?"

"I should very much like to be a soldier. Like Stephen."

"It's a noble profession." She scanned his attentive face. "Although a difficult one."

"Stephen has it in his head to send me off to school once we reach Camden, but I would hate that." He hesitated. "Would you speak to him about it for me, Tessa?"

The serious expression in his handsome golden-brown eyes so like his brother's captured her heart.

He needs me.

"I'd be honored. But, based on your past history with accidents, I would advise you not to choose artillery as your specialty," she said with a wink.

He drew back and then he snorted. "Oh, Tessa. You may be right about that."

As they continued their walk, Tessa basked in the warmth of their growing friendship and planned the best way to approach Stephen. It would indeed be sad to lose Adam so soon after they reached their destination.

Despite the dark clouds and the pungent smell of rain in the air, the weather held. They came upon a shallow stream, and as a precaution, Stephen instructed her and Adam to remain on the bank with Sally. Francis drove the wagon while Stephen held the reins of the lead horse and they made their way through the water that came halfway up the wheels. When the wagon reached the other side, Stephen came back for Tessa, pulling her up onto Knight and seating her in front of him. Once more, she leaned back against him, reveling in his closeness.

Adam followed alongside them, yanking a reluctant Sally through the knee-deep water.

Once back on the wagon, Tessa and the boys spent the

morning playing a game they created, seeing who could spy the most animals.

Around noon, they came upon a narrow lane and a sign that read *McEvans Farm, fresh strawberries*.

The thought of strawberries made Tessa's mouth water. "Stephen, they must have other vegetables too. And milk. No offense to Sally, but do you think they'd have fresh cow's milk?"

Mounted on Knight, Stephen studied her closely. What was he thinking?

She smiled her most entreating smile. "Can we not make a stop?"

"We'll stop, but let me go to the farm. We can't be sure what awaits us at the end of this lane. There's a handy turnaround right here by the road. The boys can water the horses from the barrel. We'll not start a fire, but maybe make lunch from what they have at the farm."

Tessa pouted a bit but said, "You know best. Come on, boys, let's move off the road."

Stephen waited while Francis maneuvered the wagon onto the roundabout.

Tessa hurried over to him. "You have the money from the sale of the horses?"

He tapped his waistcoat where he kept his wallet. "I do."

"Can we treat ourselves? We are all so very tired of bacon, rabbit, and squirrel. Some carrots, sweet potatoes, beets, or peas would be heavenly." She brushed her fingers across her lips. "Oh, my mouth is watering at the thought of ham and baked squash. And eggs would be grand."

He prodded Knight toward the lane and had ridden only a few yards when Tessa called out, "Peaches, Stephen. See if they have peaches. I can make a pie!"

"Hurry on, Knight, before she thinks of something else." Stephen chuckled and pushed Knight into a canter.

After watering the horses, the boys occupied themselves

trying to throw pebbles into a bucket. Tessa leaned against the open wagon backboard where she had spread some of her sketches. At the faint laughter of a child, she glanced up at the road leading to the farm. A young woman came her way holding the hand of a golden-haired toddler.

"Good morning," the woman called out, a pleasant smile on her face.

"Good morning," Tessa responded and dropped to her knees in front of the child. "What a lovely little girl. What's your name?"

"Anne," she whispered and pressed herself back into her mother's petticoats.

The woman caressed her daughter's head. "I'm Mrs. McEvans. This is our farm."

Tessa stood and curtsied. "A pleasure." Maybe the woman did not notice that she had avoided introducing herself.

"I met your husband." Mrs. McEvans giggled. "You must have had a long list."

Tessa glanced away, unwilling to correct the woman's assumption. "We'll be so happy to have some vegetables for a change. And fresh fruit."

Mrs. McEvans spotted Tessa's drawings. "My goodness, did you do these? They are very good."

"Yes, thank you."

The woman picked up one of the sketches and frowned. "I thought your husband said his name was Griffith. Yet you signed these *Harris*."

Tessa's face heated.

"You're not married, are you?" Mrs. McEvans threw down the drawing. "I can see from your face that you are not."

Tessa remained still, awaiting an onslaught.

"Have you no shame?" The woman's face distorted with disgust.

The boys dropped their stones and hurried to stand by

Tessa. Their troubled expressions made Tessa clasp her hand to her heart.

"I'd appreciate it if you'd leave our property as soon as possible. I don't want your kind around my child." She grabbed her daughter's hand and stomped back down the road, completely ignoring Stephen as he passed her by walking beside his heavily laden horse.

Shaken, Tessa ran to the other side of the wagon and curled her arms across her stomach.

The boys followed.

"What did she mean by 'your kind'?" asked Adam, holding his arms stiff by his sides.

"Boys." Stephen's voice came from the other side of the wagon. "Come around here. I want to speak with Tessa alone, and then we will talk."

The boys obeyed, but Tessa could sense their reluctance.

Stephen joined her and pressed his shoulder against hers. She covered her face with her hands.

"Talk to me, Tessa." His voice was low-pitched, controlled.

She hugged her arms across her waist. "She gathered that we aren't married. Without hearing any particulars, she treated me as if I have a disease."

He pressed a finger under her chin and tilted her face toward him. "We've done nothing wrong."

"I know that, but if I'm honest, I should have realized what our traveling together—two unmarried people—must look like to others. I have been terribly naïve. Were I on the other side of things, I might have seen the impropriety of what we are doing. My only excuse is that my grief clouded my judgement."

"I repeat—we've done nothing wrong." He motioned for her to walk ahead of him. "Let's see if we can get that across to my brothers."

The boys sat on the overturned buckets they had been playing with earlier. Unanswered questions filled their eyes.

Stephen squatted in front of them. "What happened to Tessa just now was unfortunate. And I feel it was the result of a mean spirit."

Their frowns grew more pronounced.

"How can I put this? Society has very strict rules about how men and women can be seen...alone...together. An unmarried lady, such as Tessa, is not supposed to be with a gentleman without a chaperone." He studied their faces. "You know what that is?"

Francis nodded. "Yes, I saw them when we visited Hyde Park with mother."

"Tessa and I are breaking that very strict rule by traveling together without another adult with us. It is a serious breach that can ruin a man or a woman's reputation. The tarnish could even spread to their family and friends. Mrs. McEvans believed we are behaving improperly and reacted strongly." He sighed. "Too strongly, in my opinion."

Adam clenched his fists. "She's the one who behaved improperly. She was horribly rude to Tessa."

Tessa held out her hands. "To her credit, she is a mother protecting her child. She did not want her daughter to come in contact with someone she feels is of bad reputation. That is what she meant by 'your kind.'"

Stephen stood. "I have to warn you, as we travel, we may come in contact with people who will react in a similar way. We must ignore them and pray that we will not let ourselves get angry. They won't know our circumstances or the tragedy we suffered that brought us to where we are."

His words stung Tessa's heart.

Adam stared at his oldest brother. "If you were married, we would not be having this trouble?"

What a shrewd question. Judging by Stephen's flinch, marriage wasn't an option. Was it for her?

Stephen blew out a big breath. "Let's speak of this later.

Right now, let's get these provisions loaded. We'll eat our lunch and be on our way." He grinned at her and lifted his eyebrows. "I have fresh bread and blackberry jam...and milk. I hope Sally won't be offended that it's cow's milk."

Tessa appreciated his efforts to comfort her, but the angry woman had humiliated her. She couldn't be more hurt if the woman had slapped her.

After they loaded the supplies and gathered together on the blankets, Tessa spread jam generously over slices of bread and poured milk into tin cups. She washed and sliced a handful of strawberries for each of them, licking the deliciously sweet juice from her fingers. Between the food and the looks of delight on her men's faces, her spirits improved.

Her men...that's how she saw them now, and no one, no matter how judgmental, could take that from her.

Stephen had spoken of more confrontations. How many more would she...they...have to endure?

CHAPTER 9

*A*fter lunch, they quickly left the McEvans farm. Francis and Adam rode on the wagon seat with Francis holding the reins. Knight was tethered to the backboard. Stephen invited Tessa to walk with him out of earshot.

"What are we to do?" Tessa asked. "Can we not continue as we have been and try to keep away from others and their speculations?"

"And risk a repeat of what happened today? I won't have you...or my brothers...upset again."

"But, as you have said more than once, we haven't behaved improperly."

He sighed. "In all honesty, we have. We travel in the manner of a married couple, flaunting the expected morals of society—a society in which reputation is all. Can you imagine what will be said when we arrive at Camden together? Will people genuinely want to hear about the nightmare we survived? Rumor and gossip have destroyed many lives." Misgivings clouded Tessa's eyes and twisted Stephen's insides. "Sadly, if news of our...arrangement...became known, it is you who would suffer most. As a man, I could overcome it. As a woman, you could not. It is the way of the world."

Tessa kicked a pebble and watched it skip across the trail and into the underbrush.

If only he could do something to remove her forlorn expression. Stephen stopped walking. "Jefferson suggested an answer."

She turned to him with her mouth dropping open. "You spoke to him about this?"

"He was the one who broached it. He was very fond of you and didn't want to see you harmed." Stephen hesitated, choosing his words. "He said we should marry."

Tessa's eyebrows shot up. "Marry?"

"Yes. He mentioned that the commandant of Fort Hampton could marry us." He searched her crystal-blue eyes, usually so open and honest, for any sign of abhorrence. He found nothing there but curiosity. His pulse raced. Dare he hope she was amenable?

"It would not be a church ceremony. As I'm sure, neither of us wants to stand before God and make promises in His name. That way, when we reach Camden, should we decide...we could easily dissolve the union."

She stared down at the tufts of grass growing in the center of the trail.

Had he shocked her...insulted her...with his strange idea? She was an incredibly fine woman. Talented, intelligent, caring, brave—everything he could desire in a mate. Did he want a fake marriage? And yet it felt premature to propose a real one.

"Keep up, you two," Adam yelled, leaning out of the wagon and motioning for them to hurry.

"Coming, Adam," Stephen called back. "Look at me, Tessa." When she did, he wanted to reach over and smooth the wrinkles that furrowed her lovely brow. "This is awkward. This is not the wedding you must have dreamed about. But we do like each other. Do we not?"

"Yes." She spoke the word so softly, he had to lean down to hear.

"And friendship...and admiration...make for a good relationship for us? Albeit temporary, should that come to pass."

"Yes."

Was a temporary arrangement what he truly wanted? Should he have proposed at all? He teetered as if he had one foot in a boat and one on the dock. Indecision was not something he suffered often.

"So you are amenable?" His body tensed as he anticipated her answer.

She clasped her hands at her waist and locked eyes with him. "You must give me some time."

Stephen pulled his eyes away from hers and stared at the small freckle at the base of her neck next to the shallow where her pulse fluttered. What would it feel like to caress her there?

He mentally shook himself and stepped back. "Of course. But we will arrive at the fort tomorrow."

"I'll give you my decision soon." Tessa hurried away to join the boys, who had halted the wagon.

With his senses alive to the point of pain, Stephen helped her up onto the wagon seat and then rode ahead on Knight until he came upon a narrow river. He searched the banks and found a place to cross. He tied one end of a rope to a pine tree and waded into the water that reached Knight's chest, testing the current. Upon reaching the other shore, he tied the rope around another sturdy tree, forming a guideline that would help keep the wagon on course.

The wagon reached him as he rode up the embankment. Tessa sat in between Francis and Adam, who were sharing a belly laugh. She adjusted Adam's cocked hat that was askew, and her silvery laugh echoed across the water. What a compelling sound. Another trait to add to the appealing things about her.

~

*a*s the water splashed up around Stephen, soaking his shirt that now clung to his skin, Tessa struggled not to stare. An accomplished rider, he used his long, muscular legs to guide his horse. In the war, he'd surely been a capable leader of men and a fierce warrior. He was a beautifully, wonderfully made man. Even more, he revealed a gentle, sensitive, and caring nature.

A revelation thundered its way through her consciousness.

I love him.

Breathless, she clasped her arms around her waist and barely managed to restrain her body from doubling over.

"I say, Tessa," Francis said, his expression alarmed. "Are you quite all right?"

She laughed. "Yes, I am quite all right."

Stephen called out, "Tessa, you must remain here while I lead the wagon across."

She waited on shore as he grasped the harness of the lead horse and directed the boys in maneuvering the wagon across the river, teaching them what needed to be done. With her heart full to bursting, she prayed for their safety. Her body sagged from relief when they finally settled in a clearing that would be their campsite.

Stephen returned, reached down and lifted her up, and seated her onto Knight behind him. "Hold tight. There's been no rain to speak of lately, so the current is smooth. But we must be aware and careful."

She wrapped her arms around him and could not resist resting her head against his shoulder. He mumbled something she didn't catch and prodded Knight back across the river to where the boys waited.

Shyness overwhelmed her, and for the rest of the afternoon, she skittered away each time Stephen neared. She would not look him in the eye, afraid she might reveal her feelings, but drank him in when he was not looking. He viewed her curiously several times but never made a remark.

Francis and Adam helped set up the campsite and placed the chairs and a blanket near the cook fire.

Francis wiped sweat from his face. "It's scorching. Can we go swimming?"

Stephen put down the pistol he had been cleaning. "Good idea. Tessa?"

Her face heated. "I'd love nothing better, but I have nothing to swim in."

Stephen studied her up and down. "You're about Francis's size. You can wear a pair of his breeches and a shirt. Yes?"

"All right."

"I'll get them now." Francis hurried to search through a chest in the wagon. He jumped from the wagon and showed the clothes to Tessa. "These will do, I think."

She grinned. "Yes, they will do."

Inside the wagon, she hurriedly removed her clothing and donned the breeches and shirt. When she stood before the boys and Stephen, the boys whooped.

"You could be another brother," Adam said.

Stephen snorted. "Not quite."

Tessa brushed one of her sleeves. What must she truly look like?

The boys grabbed her arms and escorted her to the river.

Stephen followed them. While Tessa and the boys swam, he attached a rope to an overhanging branch, forming a swing.

"Stellar!" Francis called out, scrambling up the riverbank.

Francis grabbed the rope and took a running leap. Midway

over the river, he let go. He flew through the air, plunged into the water, and came up sputtering.

"Next, next," Adam yelled and, mimicking his brother, leapt into the water.

Laughing and splashing each other, the boys called out, "Now you, Tessa."

Although delighted with their playfulness, she hesitated. Stephen sat on the ground beside her and removed his shoes and stockings. He sighed and playfully wriggled his toes, making her giggle. She could not help but spot a scar on his leg. It stretched from his ankle all the way up his calf to the hem of his breeches.

It must have been a terribly painful wound. Perhaps suffered in battle? There was so much about this man she did not know.

"Come on, Tessa," Adam shouted.

Shrugging off her fears, she ran, grabbed the rope, swung out and let go, but when she hit the water, she forgot to close her mouth. The water shoved its way down her throat and into her nose, and she started to choke. Panicking, she struggled against the cloying water, not sure which way was up.

Dear Lord, I'm strangling.

Just when she thought she truly might drown, Stephen's arms encircled her and raised her to the surface. She coughed and gagged and managed to spit up what felt like half the river. He carried her to shore and sat on the bank cradling her on his lap. She kept her arms wound tightly around his neck.

"You're all right, sweet one."

His face was so close...his lips a few inches from hers. She shuddered from the force of the yearnings that stunned her body. Sweet one...he called her sweet one.

"It might be best that we marry," she whispered.

~

*A*t the campsite, once they were dressed, Tessa prepared supper. The boys dominated the conversation, recounting the events of the day, the swim, and the swing Stephen had made. After supper, with the dishes cleaned and everything put away, she made such a show of concentrating on her sketching, no one bothered her.

It soon dawned on her that her subject was Stephen seated on a stool gazing at the fire. Her pencil moved across the paper forming his neck and shoulders, reminding her of how strong and muscular they felt when he held her in his lap next to the stream. Drawing the open collar of his shirt made her recall him gulping from a canteen and how the water rolled down his neck and into the dark, curly chest hairs. Penciling the light hairs of his mustache above his full lips made her wonder what his lips would feel like caressing hers.

She shook from longings that were becoming more familiar and quickly stuffed the drawing into her rucksack.

"Something amiss?" Stephen asked, stretching out his legs.

She grabbed her rucksack and stood up from her chair. "I-I —no. I'm tired. I believe I'll retire."

"I'll wish you good night, then." He spoke in a low voice.

Despite his wishes, it proved to be a disturbing night for Tessa, who spent hours struggling to stay calm and trying to find a comfortable position.

How was she to hide her true feelings from Stephen? She hated skittering around him like a scared rabbit. Would she drum up the courage to voice her love for him? Should she, since he did not love her? If the close contact with him was difficult now, how much more so would it be when they were man and wife?

She prayed for guidance before she finally succumbed to a fitful sleep.

CHAPTER 10

They arose before dawn the following morning, ate breakfast, and got back on the trail as the brilliant sun brushed the pink and purple sky with cerulean blue. Still only three-fourths of the way through Virginia, they trekked up and down rolling terrain as they skirted the foothills of the Blue Ridge Mountains until midafternoon.

Stephen and Tessa walked with Knight beside the wagon, and Adam kept Sally company at the back.

"Look there." Francis, who drove the wagon, pointed up the road. "A woman is waving at us. She seems rather frantic."

Stephen handed Knight's reins to Tessa and ran.

"Take Knight." Tessa passed the reins to Adam, who had joined them holding Sally's rope.

Just as Stephen reached the woman, she fell to her knees and sobbed. Tessa joined them, knelt beside her, and wrapped her arm across her emaciated form.

"Praise the Lord. Praise the Lord," the woman muttered, pressing her hands to her face.

The woman's skin, which hung off her bones like parchment, was gray. Her homespun dress, its color burned away by the sun and many washings, was caked in mud from the hem to her knees. She sucked in deep gulps of breath and shivered as she struggled to speak.

Was she sick?

Tessa felt her forehead. "No fever."

The woman clasped the neck of Stephen's shirt with her long, boney fingers. "Please...help. My...my husband."

Tessa massaged the woman's back. "What's your name?"

"Rosemary. Rosemary Colleton."

Tessa wiped tears from the woman's face. "I'm Tessa. Please, dear lady, how may we help?"

Francis halted the wagon beside them.

"Adam, bring a canteen." Tessa pushed Mrs. Colleton's wiry hair back from her face. Her eyes, now dilated with fear, were sky blue—the same as Tessa's.

Adam tied Knight and Sally to the backboard and returned with the canteen.

Tessa held it to the woman's parched lips. "Slowly. Just a few sips."

Mrs. Colleton moaned as the liquid trickled over her tongue and down her throat. She must be parched.

"Now, take in a deep breath." Stephen gently tugged the canteen from her grasp. "Let it out slowly."

How kind he was. And he inspired confidence. Mrs. Colleton's dilated pupils were already constricting.

Mrs. Colleton followed his instructions, then spoke through her trembling lips. "My husband. Digging well. Walls fell in. Tried all night to get him out." She grabbed Tessa's arm. "Please, can we go?"

Stephen moved to grasp her under her arms. "Are you able to stand?"

"I-I think so."

Tessa curved her arm around Mrs. Colleton's waist, and she

and Stephen lifted her to her feet. She would have toppled over, but Stephen steadied her.

"Path to our cabin." She indicated the way.

"How far?" Stephen asked.

"Half a mile."

"This lady needs our help, boys." Stephen nodded to the other side of the trail. "Over there is a good place to move off the road and settle the wagon. Hurry...fast as you can. Adam, bring me Knight, then tether the draft horses. Give them food and water. Tessa and I will go ahead. You both must follow."

The boys stared at each other, their eyes bulging.

"You can do this," Stephen encouraged them. "There's a path here, so take that. Oh, and attach our extra ropes to Knight's saddle."

Mrs. Colleton clasped the edges of her shawl. Why was she wearing it in such torrid weather? The heavy garment that draped over her shoulder and across her chest moved. What in the world?

Tessa peered down into the folds of the wrap to discover a face no bigger than the palm of her hand. "It's a baby!"

"Our little boy," Mrs. Colleton whispered and hugged him close. "Born yesterday. My milk didn't come in." A tear rolled down her cheek. "He may not last the night."

Wanting to relieve the woman's burden, Tessa held out her hands. "Please, may I take him? I promise to keep him safe."

Trembling, the new mother slowly unwrapped the shawl and handed her son to Tessa. His tiny face was pale, and his chest barely moved up and down. His spindly legs hung out of a scrap of napkin.

Tessa gasped. "I've never seen such a small infant."

Stephen led Knight over to them. "Let me help you onto my horse, Mrs. Colleton."

She nodded and he picked her up and settled her onto the stallion's back.

"Adam." Tessa pressed the infant against her heart. "Bring Sally to me, please."

They made a strange sight—Stephen in the lead, guiding Knight along the narrow, muddy path while Mrs. Colleton rode bent over on the horse's back, clinging to his neck. Tessa took up the rear, holding the baby with one hand and Sally by her rope with the other.

Their pace restricted, it took them half an hour to reach the rustic homestead comprised of a one-room cabin, a privy, a small vegetable garden, and a one-acre field of knee-high cornstalks.

"There. Henry is there." Mrs. Colleton pointed to a large pile of stones. With a heavy groan, she dismounted, and as she leaned heavily on Stephen's arm, they headed to the well.

Mrs. Colleton bent to look down into the twenty-foot hole. "Henry, help is here. Please. Please answer."

"I'm here, Rosemary. Just barely, but I'm still here," came the croaky, faint voice.

Tessa nearly wept with joy and exchanged glances with Stephen, who closed his eyes and lifted his face to the sky.

Mrs. Colleton's legs gave way. Stephen swept her up in his arms, carried her inside the cabin, and placed her on the rope-sprung bed. Tessa tied Sally to the door latch and nestled the baby into the crook of his mother's arm.

Stephen clasped Tessa's forearm and leaned in so close their foreheads almost touched. "You can manage here?"

Tessa searched his eyes and caressed his fingers that clutched her arm. "I can."

His smile lit the caramel flecks in his eyes. "Of course you can. Not sure why I asked." He tapped the tip of her nose with his finger and left the cabin.

Her chest swelled. He had confidence in her.

Tessa moved closer to the bed. "Rosemary...may I call you that?"

"Of course, Tessa."

Tessa caressed the baby's head. "And his name?"

Rosemary curled her son closer to her side. "Jacob."

"Well, then. From what you told me, we'd best get Jacob fed, and soon." She turned to the doorway. "We have Sally, but I have to confess, I have no experience whatsoever milking a goat. I don't know where to start."

Rosemary slowly leaned up on her elbow. "Bring her here. I'll tell you how."

Tessa freed the goat and pulled her onto the middle of the cabin's dirt floor.

"There's a stool and a wash pail in the corner, there." Rosemary pointed to a wooden table. "There should be some cloths next to Jacob's nappies."

Tessa retrieved the cloths from a table piled high with recently picked tomatoes, squash, and beans. Shelves above the table held spices, a bag of flour, and a can of lard. Bunches of herbs and dried flowers hung from the rafters on strings. A kettle sat on the hearth of a stone fireplace. The dirt floor had been swept, and the room was tidy and clean.

Rosemary sat up in the bed and leaned against the pillow. "Tie the goat to the bed and place the pail underneath its udder. Wet one of the cloths and wash the teat you plan to milk."

Tessa wet the cloth and then sat on the short stool next to the goat.

"After you've washed the teat, hold it gently in your hand and lace it through your fingers. Squeeze the teat with your middle finger, then your ring finger, and then your pinky. But don't pull too hard. It will hurt her. "

Her hands trembling, Tessa reached under the goat and grasped a nipple. It felt warm and squishy. She followed Rosemary's instructions. When the first stream of milk shot across the toe of her boot, she exclaimed, "Ha! Success." After a few more tugs and squirts, the bottom of the pail was covered.

Tessa patted Sally's neck. "Thank you, good girl."

Exhausted, Rosemary fell back onto the pillow.

Tessa laid the bowl on the bed and cupped her hand underneath Jacob's head. She dipped her pinky into the milk and gently pressed it against his paper-thin lips. But they barely moved. She tried again, this time pushing her finger into his mouth. He latched on and suckled.

His tongue and gums moving against her finger sent thrills down her arms. What a beautiful sensation. Would she ever experience that response with her own child? The moment she pictured Stephen leaning over her and their child, her stomach quivered. She shook her head. Theirs would be a marriage in name only. Without professions of love. Or babies.

After much coaxing, Jacob finished a tiny bit of the milk and nestled against his mother's side. Tessa found a mug, poured the remaining milk into it, and helped Rosemary sit up until she had drunk it all. She rinsed the pail, wrung out the cloth, and draped it over the shelf.

"You rest now, Rosemary." Tessa untied Sally and led her out the doorway. "I'm going to check on your husband. I promise I'll let you know what's happening." She looked back over her shoulder. Mother and son had both fallen sound asleep.

Outside, Tessa tied Sally to a nearby tree in a patch of grass and bowed her head.

Thank you, my loving and kind Lord, for Your provisions.

The goat's survival had not been an accident. The assurance made Tessa's spirits soar with gratitude.

Lord, may I ask that You extend Your mercies to Mr. Colleton?

~

*S*tephen knelt beside the well and called down, "Mr. Colleton...Henry...I'm Stephen Griffith, and these are my brothers, Francis and Adam. We're here to get you out. Is anything broken? Can you move?"

"Nothing broken, but I'm armpit-deep in rocks." The weak voice echoed from the dark pit. "I can move my hands a little... but...the water's rising."

Stephen's pulse sped. Rising water threatened everything.

"We'll move as fast as we can, Henry." Stephen reached behind him for the lantern he had lit and tied a rope around the handle. "I'm lowering a lantern. Is there something you can attach it to?"

"Broken ladder."

Stephen caught a movement out of the corner of his eye. "Adam! You're too close to the edge. Move back." The image of his brother pitching headlong into the pit clenched his chest muscles.

Halfway down the hole, the lantern illuminated Henry's gaunt face. When it came within his reach, he moaned and slowly untied it and hung it on a ladder rung.

Stephen leaned farther out over the hole. "Now, can you open up the loop I made in the rope and slip it underneath your arms?"

Groans floated up to the surface. "I can't. I can't move my arms. No feeling in 'em."

Tessa hurried across the yard and knelt beside Stephen at the lip of the well. She cupped her hands around her mouth. "Mr. Colleton, your wife and baby are resting. They are going to be fine."

"Thank God." He choked on the words.

Inches separated Stephen's body from Tessa's, but they could not have been closer in their thoughts. She had picked the right moment and the best words to encourage the desperate man.

"Give us a moment, Henry." Stephen crawled away from the edge of the pit and sat on the ground. "One of us has to go down."

"What?" Tessa clasped her chest. "Is there no other way?"

The smudges under her lovely blue eyes had darkened, and her shoulders sagged. He yearned to hug her to him.

"I'll go." Francis's voice shook.

Stephen rose up onto his knees. "I can't tell you how much that means, but I think it must be Adam. He's the smallest among us."

Panic filled Adam's eyes.

How could he reassure his younger brother? As he would a soldier about to go on a mission. Stephen had prepared many men for battle with calm, confidence, and comradery. And sharing as much information as necessary.

"We'll tie one end of a rope to Knight's saddle and the other around you. We'll lower you down, and you'll help Mr. Colleton secure the rope over his head and under his arms. First, we raise Mr. Colleton up, and then we'll pull you out. Our ropes are strong. Knight is strong, and he's never let me down before. You are strong. Mr. Colleton needs us. You can do this, Adam." Stephen clamped his hand on Adam's shoulder.

Adam stood, stiffened his arms, and clenched his fists. "If you think I can, Stephen, then I will."

Stephen swallowed hard. He'd never been more proud of, or more scared for, his younger brother.

Francis guided Knight closer and tied a rope to his saddle. He approached Adam, and before securing the other end around him, he clapped him on his shoulder. "I'm proud of you, little brother."

"Thank you, but you have to promise. If I live through this, no more jokes about my accidents and my hard head."

Francis held out his hand. "Promise."

Adam shook his hand and held up his arms for Francis to slide the noose around his body.

Stephen grabbed Adam's arm and lowered him down along the wall of the pit. "Francis, move Knight back until the rope is tight."

Knight stepped back as Francis ordered and bobbed his head.

"You ready, Adam, for us to start lowering you?" Stephen glanced at Tessa, who stood a few feet away with her head bowed. "Add my prayers to yours, Tessa. Please."

She nodded and folded her hands.

Adam tugged on the rope. "I'm ready."

With his back so tight with tension Stephen thought his spine might crack, he gripped the rope as, inch by inch, Francis prodded Knight forward until Adam called out, "I'm here, standing on the rocks next to Mr. Colleton."

"Good job, Adam," Stephen said. "Now, take the rope that we sent down with the lantern and tie the loop around Mr. Colleton's back and underarms."

"I will," Adam yelled, "but some of the rocks are falling, and the water has reached Mr. Colleton's shoulders." There was a pause. "It's mighty tight down here."

Stephen gritted his teeth. "Soldier on, Adam, fast as you can."

The wait for Adam's next words dried Stephen's mouth until he could barely swallow.

"He's ready. Start pulling."

Keeping tension on the rope, Francis guided Knight back, farther and farther until Stephen ordered him to stop.

As close to the edge as he dared, Stephen reached down into the hole and twisted Mr. Colleton's body to face the wall. He clasped him underneath his arms. "Two more steps, Francis," he ordered and pulled with all his might.

Mr. Colleton slid out of the pit gasping for air but lay still on the ground.

"Francis, come help drag him away. Untie the rope from Knight and then tie this one in its place." Stephen handed him the rope. "Fast as you can."

Tessa knelt beside Mr. Colleton. "I'll help Mr. Colleton roll away, Stephen. You get started pulling Adam back up. I'll not wait much longer to kiss his beautiful face."

"Yes, ma'am."

Would she kiss *him* when this is over? Not a good time for those thoughts. *Concentrate on the mission at hand.*

When Knight was readied, Stephen gripped the rope again. "We're pulling now, Adam."

"None too soon, brother. More rocks are falling, and one just hit me on my shoulder."

Stephen quashed the panic that rose up in his parched throat. "Count to ten and you'll be out of there."

"One Two. Ouch! Three. Four..." Adam's voice shook.

Adam reached the top of the pit at the same time he reached ten. Stephen pulled him out and lay beside him on the ground a few moments before he could move or speak. He gasped for air and struggled to disguise how the rescue had shaken him.

Francis slid down beside them and clasped his younger sibling to him. "Wahoo! You did it, little brother. And you, big brother. And you, Knight."

"And me! Well, my prayers." Tessa knelt beside them, and trembling, she curved her hands around Adam's cheek and kissed his forehead, his eyelids, and his mouth. "Thank God. Thank God."

Stephen's body stopped shaking just as Tessa kissed Adam's mouth. What would those lovely lips feel like on his?

When Francis slapped Adam on his back, Adam yelped. "Ouch! That hurts. It's where a rock fell on me."

Francis grinned. "Wouldn't have hurt so much if it had fallen on your—"

Adam held up his pointer finger. "Remember your promise."

"Right." Francis pursed his lips.

Relieved and overjoyed, Stephen threw his head back and laughed. They all gathered in a circle and hugged each other like family.

Should he consider making them a real family? Would Tessa want that?

CHAPTER 11

$\mathcal{T}$he next two days presented so many challenges that each night, everyone dropped onto their pallets, spent. Stephen and the boys worked on the well, shoring up the sides with rocks and building a wall from which to suspend a bucket. The boys cut and split firewood that they piled near the cabin. They traveled back and forth between the homestead and the wagon to check on the draft horses. Tessa gathered the ripening vegetables from the garden and made a stew.

Rosemary, Jacob, and Henry cuddled in the bed together, presenting such a sweet picture that Tessa started sketching them. During the quiet time she spent with them, she shared her story of how she came to be traveling with Stephen and his brothers. Neither of them said a harsh word, nor did they pass judgement.

The morning of their third day with the Colletons, after breakfast, Tessa and Stephen met at a blackberry thicket she had discovered at the edge of the woods near the vegetable garden.

The berries grew so abundantly, she filled her pail within minutes.

Stephen picked a couple of the plump berries and popped them into his mouth. "My, that's good."

A tiny spot of juice wet the corner of his lips, and he licked it with his tongue. The natural gesture sent waves of sensation through Tessa's body. His every movement—striding across the yard, stretching his arms over his head, the bulge of his biceps when picking up a heavy stone, his long legs guiding Knight over a stream—intensified those sensations to the point that she found herself avoiding eye contact lest he guess her feelings.

He folded his arms across his chest. "Is something amiss, Tessa?"

"I—" She reached for a berry, and a sticker dug into her skin. "Ouch!"

He took the pail from her, set it on the ground, and held her hand. "Let me see."

He pulled his kerchief from around his neck and swabbed the speck of blood from her skin. He pressed his warm lips to the scratch, and Tessa lost her breath for a moment.

"Better?" he asked, still bowed over her hand and looking up at her.

She tugged her hand away and focused on the blackberry bush. "I should rub some of the leaves on it. They make a fine astringent."

The moment the leaves touched the scratch, they burned like fire. Just what she needed to gain some self-control.

Stephen picked up the pail and led the way back to the cabin.

"How much longer should we stay here, Stephen?" She matched her steps with his.

"Whenever they seem ready to take care of themselves again. I bow to your judgement."

He valued her opinion.

"Jacob is thriving. His skin has turned a healthy pink, as has

Rosemary's. Henry says the feeling in his arms and legs has returned." They stopped in front of the cabin, and she rubbed her neck. "Let's see how well he moves about today. If he's strong on his feet, then I say we get back on the trail tomorrow."

"A sound plan." Stephen headed toward where Knight was tethered near the woods.

Tessa paused in the cabin doorway.

Had they made the right decision to marry? Stephen was a wonderful man. Any woman would be blessed to love and marry him. When the time came, would a divorce...or annulment...or dissolution...or whatever they chose to call it put such a stain on his reputation that no one would want him? No. A woman who truly loved him could easily understand his gallantry.

What would a divorce...a failed marriage...do to her own standing as well as prospects for getting commissions? It would take the gossip of only one malicious person to damage her reputation beyond repair.

~

That evening after supper, everyone gathered outside the cabin to watch the sunset that splashed brilliant reds, oranges, and yellows across the gray sky. Tessa's fingers itched to grab a canvas, and her mind sorted through the colors she would need to recreate the breathtaking view. She and Rosemary, who cuddled Jacob in her lap, rocked in chairs Henry had fashioned out of willow branches. Stephen and Henry sat on benches made of tree limbs resting on stones. The boys had built a fire, not for warmth since the air sizzled, but for gazing. They crouched nearby, talking and poking the flames.

Henry put down his pipe and held his arms out to Tessa and Stephen. "Dear friends, I cannot thank you enough for everything you have done for Rosemary and me. You saved our lives. I know beyond a doubt that God sent you in answer to our prayers. I also know that it was no accident that Sally survived the horrible massacre. It was God's foresight. Her milk saved our little Jacob."

Tessa's sentiments exactly. She sucked in a breath, and tears pooled in her eyes. She caught Stephen's glance, and they shared a smile.

"You are more than welcome, Henry." Stephen glanced at his brothers. "Tessa and I are honored by your friendship, and we hate to go, but we talked about it and feel we must get back on the trail and make our way to Camden."

Rosemary curled her fingers around Tessa's hand that rested on the arm of the rocking chair. "I hate to see you go too." She leaned in close to Tessa and whispered, "I'm glad you shared your troubles with us. I don't judge you and never will, but I feel it's a good thing that you and Stephen will marry at the fort." She glanced at Stephen and Henry, who were engaged in a lively conversation. "Because if you didn't...you've another four or five weeks before you reach Camden. People can be cruel. There are some women who live on gossip. They won't wait for an explanation of why you and Stephen came together. I can't bear the thought of you being the object of such ugliness." She squeezed Tessa's hand and grinned. "Besides, four or five weeks of resisting such a magnificent man would wear down the most fervently faithful lady."

"He is magnificent, is he not?"

"Yes, but Henry mustn't hear me say so."

Her words sent them into giggles that caught Mr. Colleton's attention.

"Rosemary, why don't you sing for us?" Henry knocked his pipe against his boot and dumped the ashes out onto the ground. "I'll fetch your dulcimer."

When he returned with the instrument, Rosemary handed

Jacob to Tessa, who cuddled him in her arms. Tessa nuzzled his nose. He smelled of goat's milk and a lovely sweetness she did not recognize. She laid his soft, warm body on her chest and rocked, marveling at the tiny heartbeat that fluttered next to hers.

Rosemary struck the first haunting chord, sending chills down Tessa's arms. When she began singing "When I Survey the Wondrous Cross," the boys ambled over and sat on the bench with Stephen. Francis pulled his harmonica from his waistcoat and played along. Henry was the first to accompany Rosemary's singing, and soon everyone joined in.

Jacob sighed his contentment, and Tessa kissed his head.

Family. Would she ever have it? Could she and Stephen experience a real marriage?

Stephen stared at her, his eyes ablaze with something she could not discern. Yearning?

They needed to talk.

CHAPTER 12

*T*hey woke at dawn the next morning to a day that promised to be clear and hot. After breakfast, they bid a tearful goodbye to the Colletons. When Tessa presented Rosemary with a drawing of her little family cuddled together in their bed, the woman cried even more.

Tessa, reliving the intimate family gathering from the night before and needing time to sort her thoughts, walked beside the wagon rather than sitting with the boys. Stephen rode Knight and kept yards ahead. Had he sensed her desire for solitude?

The day passed without incident. They stopped for lunch and twice more to rest the horses. Come evening, they camped in a clearing next to a softly gurgling stream. After a supper of rabbit stew, fresh vegetables, and biscuits that Rosemary had sent along with them, Tessa and the boys washed the dishes. When they finished, the young men chattered beside the campfire eating blackberries out of mugs. Just as she put the last dish in a chest, Stephen approached.

"We need to talk."

"We must talk."

They spoke the words together.

Stephen swept out his arm, and she followed him to the creek. Once there, she sat on a moss-covered rock, and he remained standing.

"Tessa, we haven't spoken in some time about getting married, and I want to be clear about it."

"So do I." She leaned back. "First, though, will you sit? It's hurting my neck looking up at you."

She scooted over and he sat beside her, so close their hips touched.

He rested his arms on his legs. "Are you still committed to marrying?"

She stared at the water that danced over layers of rocks on its way downstream. In places, here and there, the surface mirrored the sunset's pinks and oranges.

"If I'm honest, I have swayed back and forth." She angled her knees toward him. "Should we bow to convention or defy it? What are the chances people will find out that we've traveled together without the benefit of marriage?"

He faced her. "Do you want to take that chance? Because I do not. For me, it isn't only the two of us who would be damaged by gossip. I don't want my brothers' lives tainted in any way."

Tessa tucked in her chin. "I needed reminding of that."

"My brothers have grown very fond of you, Tessa." He covered her hand with his. "If you are hurt, they will be hurt." He paused. "As I would."

She relished the comfort and warmth of his hand on hers. "But what of divorce? That doesn't sit well with society either."

He rubbed his thumb across her fingers. Was he aware of what that small movement did to her pulse?

"I spoke to Henry Colleton of that very thing. He told me that he and his wife indentured themselves in Charles Town for seven years. Their master was a barrister, and through him,

Henry became aware of several divorces. It is more prevalent in the colonies than you would imagine."

"Rosemary never mentioned being an indentured servant."

Stephen scowled. "Their master was abusive. It's something they wish to forget."

Rosemary and Henry were able to endure something terrible together because their marriage was based on love. Tessa yearned for that kind of steadfast commitment.

"It seems desertion is the most common ground for divorce, but the second is annulment, which is what we would seek."

Tessa stared at the rushing water once again. She pursed her lips. "I bow to your judgement, Stephen."

He stood and assisted her to stand in front of him. "So...we agree to go through with the civil ceremony?"

She filled her lungs with air and let it out slowly. "Agreed."

~

*M*idafternoon of the following day, they entered the gates of Fort Hampton. The guard instructed them to position their wagon toward the back of the grounds next to the log fence that encircled the three-acre garrison.

During his stint in the army, Stephen had often bivouacked in similar places. As they rode through, he took note of the main building. Situated in the center of the fort, the single-story wooden structure housed the commandant's office that he would visit as soon as they settled the wagon. Two smaller buildings—more than likely housing for the officers and their wives—buttressed the main building on either side. Two-man tents dotted the area to the east of the headquarters. Other structures included a stockade, a corral for the cavalry and draft horses, a shed for the blacksmith, and a small trading post. From the number of guards and soldiers going about their tasks, he estimated the fort housed around two hundred men.

He joined Tessa and his brothers by the wagon. After caring for the horses, the boys shuffled from foot to foot, eager to explore their new surroundings. Tessa nervously twirled her fingers around the end of her braid.

"Boys, take Knight over to the corral and ask the person in charge if he would curry and feed him. Here's money to pay." He tossed a coin to Francis. "When you return, start a fire and help Tessa with whatever she needs to make supper. I'll change and head for the commandant's office."

He entered the wagon and found a waistcoat and a pristine cravat in one of the chests. Back outside, he donned the coat, tied the cravat, and strapped his sword around his waist.

Tessa stepped close and adjusted his cravat. "You look handsome."

"Thank you." Did she know how lovely she looked? Even after a morning on the wagon trail, her eyes shone bright blue and her cheeks glowed. The sprinkle of freckles on her nose begged to be caressed. He curled his hand around hers. "Are you certain this is what you want?"

She steeled her back. "I'm certain."

Her firm response spurred him onward, and he covered the distance to the headquarters building in a few long strides.

The guard at the door, dressed in a flawless uniform of buff pants and red coat and brandishing a musket, stood to attention. He studied Stephen from head to toe, taking a second glance at his sword. "State your business, sir."

"I'm Stephen Griffith. I'd like to report an Indian attack, and I must also address the commandant on a personal matter."

The guard entered the office and returned moments later. "Colonel Stanton will see you."

Stephen followed him into the office and confronted the commandant, who was seated at his desk in a meticulously tailored uniform the highly polished buttons of which flashed when he stood to bow. His white wig tied back with a black bow did not have a hair out of place. The chiseled features of his face and the deep lines around his mouth and eyes purveyed strength.

Stephen returned the man's bow.

The colonel motioned to a chair facing the desk. "Please be seated, Mr. Griffith."

Stephen sat and waited.

"The sword you carry... You served in the army?"

"Royal Horse Guards."

"Blues?" The colonel leaned forward, eyes wide. "Fine regiment. Proud history. Rank?"

"Lieutenant. I gave up my commission to care for my brothers after our mother died."

The colonel sat back and folded his hands in his lap. "How may I assist you?"

"Two things. A week ago, the wagon train I traveled with was attacked by Indians. It was a terrible massacre. I was several miles away helping fellow travelers, the Harrises—a man and his daughter—whose wagon wheel had broken." Stephen clamped his jaw shut as visions of the massacre bludgeoned his mind.

"Tragic, indeed. But strange." The colonel shuffled the papers in front of him. "We've had no reports of an Indian uprising."

"My brothers and I buried the bodies. Eighteen victims. Miss Harris, my brothers, and I are the only survivors."

"Ghastly business. We have Cherokee scouts attached to our regiment. I'll send them out." The colonel rested his arms on the desk. "And the personal matter?"

Stephen cleared his throat, then hesitated. What he was about to say would change his life forever.

"Mr. Griffith?" the colonel prodded. "Your personal matter?"

"Uh, yes, sir. Miss Harris and I wish to be married. Can you...would you...perform the ceremony?"

The colonel raised an eyebrow. "She survived the attack... alone...and has been with you since?"

Stephen bristled. "Yes, sir."

"Quite a story the two of you must have." His eyes softened. "I'd be honored. And I'm certain Mrs. Stanton would be overjoyed to take part in a wedding." He walked around his desk. "Sergeant Mayfield," he called out.

The sergeant opened the door. "Sir?"

"Ask Mrs. Stanton to join us."

"Sir." The sergeant clicked his heels and left.

The colonel sat on the corner of his desk facing Stephen. "Marriage is a solemn undertaking. I won't ask any particulars, but from what I gather, this marriage is a form of chivalry?"

"Miss Harris is a fine gentlewoman for whom I have the highest regard."

"That answers my question better than a yes or no."

As the door opened and Mrs. Stanton entered, Stephen and the colonel stood side by side. Soft tendrils of hair—once red but now muted by gray—curled out from her pristine white mobcap and framed her sweet round cheeks. Her lively brown eyes bespoke someone who laughed often.

She looked from Stephen to her husband and rested her arms in front of her thick waist. "Henry? Is something amiss?"

"Not at all, my dear. As a matter of fact, I have news which will be of delight to you. There is to be a wedding."

Mrs. Stanton's worried expression changed into a beam that lit her face. "That is fine news, husband."

The colonel winked at Stephen. "I knew you would be pleased. This is Mr. Griffith. Mr. Griffith, my wife."

Stephen bowed and Mrs. Stanton curtsied, her eyes full of curiosity.

"Mr. Griffith and his...intended...Miss Harris have asked me to perform their marriage ceremony. As I will be leaving tomorrow with a part of the garrison, the ceremony will have to take place this evening. Say, seven?" He aimed the question at Stephen.

The statement dazed him for a moment.

Seven? This was well and truly happening.

"Only three hours, Henry?" Mrs. Stanton exclaimed.

The colonel approached her and tapped her cheek with his finger. "I have all faith in you, Katherine. Go see what you can do for these young people."

The smile she sent him expressed her love and admiration. The momentary exchange gave Stephen a heartwarming glimpse into a marriage between two people who were meant for each other. Once again, doubts about his choices roiled in his mind. Could a marriage succeed when only one person loved the other?

Mrs. Stanton wound her arm around Stephen's. "I'm eager to meet your Miss Harris. I won't pry about the particulars, but I am curious about why you have asked my husband to officiate."

"Mrs. Stanton, your generosity and kindness amaze me. I don't want to seem ungrateful, but the fewer people who know the particulars—as you call them—the better."

She chortled. "You do know that what you said just now has piqued my curiosity even more." Her expression turned serious. "Please know that once I wheedle *the particulars* from my husband, your secret will be safe with me."

Stephen tucked her arm closer. "You are a prize, Mrs. Stanton."

Arm in arm, they strolled to the wagon, where Stephen made introductions. "Mrs. Stanton, this is Miss Harris, and these are my brothers, Francis and Adam."

Mrs. Stanton clasped both her hands around one of Tessa's. "I'm very pleased to meet you. What a lovely bride you will make. And what handsome men you have about you."

Adam poked Francis with his elbow. "She must mean me."

Francis poked him back.

Mrs. Stanton released Tessa's hand. "But you must call me Katherine."

The wrinkles across Tessa's brow softened at the woman's warm greeting.

"I am Tessa," she responded shyly.

Mrs. Stanton clapped her hands. "We must get down to it. We have only three hours—"

Tessa's eyebrows shot upward. "So soon?"

Stephen wanted to reassure her, but his words would not come.

"Lieutenant Baxton and his wife are visiting their daughter and new granddaughter in Charles Town, South Carolina, which leaves their quarters free." Mrs. Stanton smiled. "I'm certain they would be happy to have you as their guests for your honeymoon. Boys, you will stay with the colonel and me in our guestroom. Do you have proper attire?"

"Yes, ma'am." They echoed each other.

"Then you, Mr. Griffith, and your brothers may prepare for the wedding in our guestroom. Tessa, do you have a dress?"

Tessa grimaced. "I do, but it must be terribly wrinkled."

Mrs. Stanton clicked her tongue. "Not to worry. You point out the things you need, and Mr. Griffith and the boys will carry them with us to the Baxtons' quarters."

~

*A*s Mrs. Stanton bustled her away, Tessa glanced back over her shoulder at Stephen, whose stern expression revealed none of the panic that made her heart race. Upon reaching the barracks, she noticed two Indian men leaving the commandant's office. She had never seen an Indian up close and, completely fascinated, she stood still and allowed her artist's eye full rein.

She would need raw and burnt sienna and a tiny bit of yellow or umber to replicate the hues of their reddish-brown skin. Handsome men, they had angular faces, high cheekbones, and hooked, full noses. Their heads were shaved except for scalp locks embellished with hawk feathers. She admired the way both of them sprang up and slid their legs across their horses' backs, mounting in one fluid motion. When they rode past, one stared down at her, his hooded, almond-shaped eyes creating an air of mystery. Her fingers itched for her canvas and paints.

But wait. It was savages like these who killed her father.

"You've gone quite pale." Mrs. Stanton placed her arm around Tessa's waist.

"I'm fine. Maybe a little shaken by all that has occurred."

"Let's hurry inside, then."

Before long, Tessa was seated in front of a vanity mirror in the Baxtons' bedroom.

"Try to eat at least one of the biscuits, dear," Mrs. Stanton cajoled. "And finish that Bohea tea. It is difficult to come by. I do hope Mrs. Baxton remembers to bring a supply when she returns. She was so flustered about the birth of her first grandchild and packing for her journey, I don't believe she heard half of what I was saying."

She checked the hem of Tessa's dress that was lying across the bed and then stood behind Tessa and addressed her in the mirror. "Do you and Mr. Griffith want children? The colonel and I wanted them. Many, in fact. But the Lord had other plans for us. And as we know, His plans are much better for us than any we can envision."

Having children with Stephen. Tessa pictured him cradling their son in his tan, muscular arms. He would make an amazing father. And what of the intimacy that would create a child? The thought stirred her insides and she trembled. What folly. She shouldn't dream such things. Stephen didn't feel that way about her. They would marry and then end the marriage in Camden. Or would they? Had they not, without actually saying the words, left the door open to continuing their marriage?

Tessa stared at her reflection as her cheeks turned beet red. "I-I...we...haven't spoken about it."

"All in good time." Mrs. Stanton reached for a brush and made a long stroke through Tessa's tresses. "Now, let us arrange your hair. The color and texture are a glory. Let's braid some of it at the sides of your face and allow the rest to flow down your back. I had one of the corporals fetch these pink rosebuds from my garden. Won't they be lovely?"

While Mrs. Stanton fussed, Tessa treasured memories of Stephen that had culminated in the moment she realized she was in love with him. Once married, would she allow him to know how she adored him? Or should she hide her feelings and guard her heart? She could picture nothing more painful than loving a man who did not reciprocate.

Mrs. Stanton chattered the entire time she helped Tessa don her dress and tie the ribbons at the back of the bodice. The white stockings, fastened with satin streamers around her thighs, were new. The pink shoes, although a bit too large, complemented the dress. The beautiful accessories had belonged to Mrs. Stanton's sister who had tired of the rustic colonial society and moved back to England.

"There, what a lovely sight you are. Your eyes are fairly glowing. It's time." Mrs. Stanton's final words broke through Tessa's reverie.

Tessa viewed her reflection, but all she saw was moisture pooling in her eyes.

"Tears, my dear?"

"I wish my father and mother were here," she murmured. "I miss them so."

"Oh, my. I had not thought of that. I am so sorry. Of course you miss them. But you will have your husband to care for you now. And what a fine-looking, capable man he seems. Quite swoon worthy." She giggled. "Almost as handsome as my colonel."

Tessa clutched the single pink long-stemmed rose Mrs. Stanton handed her and braced her shoulders.

I am to be married. Is it what You wish for us, Lord?

CHAPTER 13

"*F*rancis, that is my cravat." Adam tried yanking the necktie from his brother as they finished dressing in the Stantons' guestroom.

"I beg your pardon. The one on the bed is yours. You know, with the jelly stain on the tip of it?"

"I...yes. You are right," Adam said, his cheeks a fiery red.

Stephen, who sat on the edge of the bed, slid his buff-colored breeches legs into his knee-length boots. He stood and, looking in the vanity mirror, adjusted the epaulets of his dark-blue coat. "You must promise me you'll both be on your best behavior. If not for my sake, then for Tessa's. As you will soon discover, weddings are very special occasions for the ladies."

Francis finished tying his cravat. "I say, Stephen, you cut a fine figure in your uniform."

Stephen snapped his heels and bowed his head. "I thank you, sir."

Adam tucked the jelly-stained end of his cravat into his waistcoat. "It's been years since I last saw you in it. Do you ever regret giving up the army?"

"I do miss it occasionally, but it means more to be with the two of you."

Adam smiled wistfully. "Mother was so proud of you. She worried, too, when you were in the thick of it."

"She was a special lady. She was proud of all her boys. And speaking of fine figures, both of you look grand." Stephen tucked his gloves into the sash draped across his chest. "I believe it's time."

Adam stopped at the guestroom doorway. "Francis, we are to have a sister." A huge smile lit his face.

"That we are," Francis answered.

As they moved toward the entrance of the Stantons' quarters, Stephen wrestled with his doubts. Was he doing his brothers a disservice by not telling them about the temporary nature of the marriage agreement? But how could he explain it to them when he didn't know his own feelings yet?

Outside, they walked along the porch that stretched across the officers' quarters and the main building. A guard ushered them into the colonel's office where the ceremony was to take place. The colonel's desk had been moved up against a window on the far side of the room. It was covered with a white tablecloth laden with a cake and dishes of food and a vase of pink roses. The plank floor had been cleared and polished to a high sheen.

A hand clasped Stephen's shoulder. "You ready?"

Stephen turned to greet the colonel and his wife. "As I'll ever be."

"Let us begin, then. The two of you, along with Adam, will situate yourselves in front of the desk, facing the door." Mrs. Stanton motioned to Francis. "Young man, you will escort Tessa from the door to where the colonel and your brothers are standing. So come with me."

Stephen stood with the colonel and Adam. Could the pounding of his heart be heard by the others? He had not felt this much panic since waiting on the battlefield for a fight to commence.

Six soldiers, immaculate in dress uniforms, strode into the room and formed an aisle. Mrs. Stanton entered, walked the aisle, and stopped opposite Stephen.

When Tessa stepped into the room, escorted by Francis, all else ceased to exist for Stephen.

What a lovely woman.

The pale-pink satin and the matching rosebuds in her silky hair gave her an air of daintiness. Stephen felt once again an impulse to shelter and care for her.

She glanced at him and then kept her head lowered as she walked down the aisle until she pressed her shoulder against his and looked up at him.

Captivated by her sparkling eyes, he did not register anything the colonel said until Francis leaned over and whispered, "You must respond with a 'yes,' brother."

"Yes, brother." Stephen swallowed hard. "I-I mean...yes."

A distinct twinkle lit Tessa's eyes, and when prompted, she whispered her response. "Yes."

The colonel held his arms out. "With the power vested in me by His Majesty King George the Second and by Willem Anne van Keppel, second earl of Albemarle, governor of Virginia, I pronounce you man and wife."

Stephen leaned down and kissed Tessa's cool lips, drinking in the lovely aroma of roses that permeated the air around her.

Though Tessa's mouth felt cool, her bottom lip was plump and soft. What a pleasure it would be to nibble on it. A sensuous pain shot through his body so strong he thought he might drown. He slid his arms around her and pulled her in tightly as if she were a lifeline. He kissed her mouth, this time with barely contained passion. Her body trembled in his embrace, and she pressed her hands against his chest.

You've frightened her. Control yourself.

"Huzzah! Huzzah! Huzzah!" the cadre shouted as they raised their swords to form an arch.

Everyone clapped and offered their congratulations, giving Stephen time to recover.

Walking underneath the arch, he whispered to Tessa, "May I know what was so amusing in the ceremony?"

Tessa giggled. "Oh, Stephen, I thought I was the only one nervous, but when you answered, 'Yes, brother,' my heart felt light again."

He grinned. "Ha! It may be a while before the boys stop teasing me about that."

They returned to the table where they cut the cake using Stephen's highly polished sword. Mrs. Stanton plated slices of the cake and offered it to the soldiers. The boys dove into the dainty ham biscuits and a bowl of fresh peaches, watermelons, and strawberries.

A soldier entered the room playing an accordion, and Stephen held out his hand to Tessa. "May I have the honor of this dance, Mrs. Griffith?"

"With pleasure, husband."

Husband. The charade daunted him. Could he survive the next few weeks without touching her, making her his own?

When she came to him, Stephen marveled at how well they fit together. He slid his arm from her waist to her back and guided her around the room through the simple footwork of a country dance. The colonel and Mrs. Stanton shared the dance and laughed when Francis and Adam swept past them in a jaunty imitation of the bride and groom.

As the evening wore on, Stephen adjusted to his decision to marry. It certainly seemed good for the boys, who each in turn gallantly approached Tessa for a dance. When they were not dancing or eating, his brothers chatted lightheartedly with the soldiers.

As his wife, Tessa no longer provided a target for scandal

and rumors. What of the intimate part of marriage? With the option of divorce looming, intimacy would be out of the question. Tessa stirred his blood as no other woman in his life. There had been times when they came close to one another that he sensed her attraction for him. Could he resist the temptation?

This would not be an easy arrangement.

After several more dances, Tessa's shoulders drooped.

Stephen held out his hand to her. "You are tired. I think it may be a good time for us to leave."

She clasped his hand as they approached their hosts.

"Colonel...Mrs. Stanton..." Stephen bowed. "Tessa and I will never forget your generosity and kindness. You have our heartfelt gratitude. Everyone, this has been a most pleasant occasion, but we must bid you good evening."

Francis and Adam hurried to Tessa and would have bowed, but she reached out and embraced them. "I am your sister now, and you may hug me whenever you please."

When she kissed them on their foreheads, Stephen gripped the hilt of his sword.

Maybe this marriage would prove to be a good decision, after all.

CHAPTER 14

Outside the colonel's office, Tessa leaned forward against the porch bannister and breathed in the cool night air. They would leave here for the honeymoon bedroom. She gulped. She needed a few more minutes. "Could we walk for a while?"

Stephen offered his arm, and they stepped off the porch and headed across the compound that was shrouded in darkness except for lanterns placed at the front gate and at numerous guard stations. This late in the evening, most of the troops had retired, but some had settled near the campfires polishing boots and cleaning muskets. They did not converse much, but when they did, they kept their voices low.

Tessa touched the rosebuds in her hair. "What a lovely occasion. So much more than I had anticipated."

"I imagine it isn't what you planned."

"Maybe not what I considered as a very young person, but it was beautifully sweet. I did miss the hymns one usually hears at weddings." She pressed the pulse at the base of her neck to stop the fluttering. "Everyone I care about was there, except for my parents." Without warning, she choked up. "Oh, dear. Where did that come from?"

He offered her his handkerchief.

She dabbed her tears and fanned her face with the fine linen cloth. "Please. Forgive me. It's been an emotional day."

"I understand." He spoke softly. "I might join you, were it allowed."

This tiny glimpse into her husband's character intrigued her. "So, as a man, you feel compelled to hide your emotions?"

"They were trained out of us, I'm afraid. Not the emotions themselves, but any display of them."

How painful that training must have been.

Tessa studied him from head to toe and relived the moment she entered the doorway for the ceremony. Standing tall and resplendent in his dress uniform, he had tied his hair back with a ribbon and draped the queue over the back of his high gold-and-red collar. His dark-blue coat was tailored to perfection, accentuating his broad shoulders and trim waist. The sight of him had so stunned her, she had kept her eyes lowered as she walked the aisle.

Mrs. Stanton's description had been correct. He *was* swoon worthy. She did so wish to paint him like that one day.

They neared the stables, and one of the horses whinnied.

"I'd like to see how Knight is faring, if we may?" Stephen asked.

"Certainly."

They entered the stables, and a young man immediately approached. "May I help you?"

"I'm here to see my horse. The black one there." Stephen pointed to Knight.

"Finest horse I ever took care of." The stable hand ran his hand across Knight's shoulder and regarded Stephen's uniform. "I see he was wounded. With a sword? In battle?"

Stephen traced the scar with his fingertips, and the muscles quivered visibly underneath. "Yes. We have experienced much together, haven't we, my fine fellow?"

Knight tossed his head and snorted.

Tessa thought back to the time at the river when she had noticed the scar along Stephen's leg. From the position of Knight's scar, they must have been wounded at the same time —one continuous wound across Stephen's leg and down Knight's shoulder.

What terrible trials had they endured—this man and the horse he so obviously loved. She shuddered.

Thank you, Lord, for bringing them both through the horrors of war.

Stephen patted Knight's neck. "We'll see you tomorrow."

They exited the stables, and one of the officers strode toward them. His uniform was spotless, and his polished sword reflected the light from the lantern suspended from the stable door.

"Good evening," he said, bowing to each of them. "I'm Lieutenant Parks. May I wish you happy, Mr. and Mrs. Griffith?"

Stephen bowed. "Thank you, sir."

"If I may, there is something this way I think you might wish to see." He swept his arm toward one of the four bastion towers at each corner of the fort.

Stephen pressed his fingertips into the small of Tessa's back. "Tessa? You aren't too tired?"

Her curiosity piqued, she shook her head.

"Lead on," Stephen replied, curling Tessa's arm through the crook of his elbow.

They came to the base of the triangular-shaped fortification and three flights of stairs. The lieutenant preceded them and signaled to the guard to let them pass. Stephen secured Tessa's arm as she lifted her skirts to mount the steps. The climb was steep, and by the time they reached the top, she was spent.

"Here we are." The lieutenant motioned toward a metal cone-shaped tube attached to a stand.

"A telescope," Tessa exclaimed. "The captain of the ship we traveled on to the colonies had one, but he wouldn't allow anyone but himself to touch it."

Grinning, the lieutenant directed the telescope toward a point in the sky. "You are in for a rare sighting. Venus and Jupiter are aligning."

"May I, please?" Tessa could barely contain her excitement, but when she walked up to the telescope, it was mounted too high for her.

"Here, this will help." The lieutenant slid a packing crate over for Tessa to stand on.

With Stephen hovering close behind her, she put an eye up to the lens. "I don't see anything."

"Let me adjust it." The lieutenant tilted the scope slightly.

Tessa blinked, and two distinct lights came into focus. "Oh, my! What am I seeing, lieutenant?"

"The larger light is Venus and the smaller one to the west of it is Jupiter."

"It is wondrous. It seems as if they will collide."

"It does, but in truth, they are millions of miles away from each other."

"Stephen, you look." Tessa spun around and found herself nose to nose with him and felt his warm breath on her lips.

She yearned to twine her arms around his neck but refrained, reminding herself that he was hers but not hers.

Holding onto her waist and gently moving her to the side, Stephen stepped up to the scope. "Fascinating. I can't thank you enough for sharing this with us. What a nice wedding memory we have made."

Tessa smiled at the lieutenant. "Yes, thank you, Lieutenant Parks. Should I live to a hundred, I won't forget this."

"My pleasure. And now, I'll go and get back to my rounds."

He descended the stairs, leaving Tessa and Stephen alone.

She stepped forward and leaned against the bastion wall and gazed up at the stars. "'Tis all beyond my comprehension —that our Lord created the heavens and now has given man the knowledge to create such instruments as this to study it."

Stephen moved close behind her. "As you said before, it is wondrous."

She spotted a tiny light in the distance floating toward them. Soon that light became ten, then twenty, then more than she could count. Her heart raced. "Look! Fireflies. Hundreds... no... thousands of them."

The greenish-yellow glowing creatures surrounded them and floated past, wave upon wave dancing across the compound. Soldiers started popping out of their tents, holding out their arms and twirling around, marveling at what they beheld. Several guards ran up the stairs and joined Tessa and Stephen. No one said a word but watched silently as nature's tiny lanterns paraded past and disappeared into the forest.

Tessa reached back and pulled Stephen's arm around her. When he circled his other arm around her also, a thrill ran through her. Her heart might burst with the emotions tumbling around in it.

Dear Lord, thank You for this magnificent gift, but what is Your plan for us?

CHAPTER 15

*S*itting on the vanity chair in the Baxtons' bedroom, Tessa pulled off her shoes and stockings and wiggled her toes. She removed the rosebuds from her hair and loosened the braids. She scrubbed her fingers through the waist-length tresses and then lifted her arms up in a long-awaited stretch. Bone tired, she yawned.

What a day, filled with every emotion imaginable. Mrs. Stanton's efforts made what could have been a sterile, businesslike transaction into a lovely, sweet occasion. The dance with Stephen in his uniform had stirred sensations that rolled over and over inside. The boys dressed in their best attire provided special, heart-tugging moments—Francis acting as escort and Adam as best man. The telescope...the fireflies.

The blessed day had begun with trepidation, doubts, and questions. And now at the end of it, she was Mrs. Stephen Griffith and the sister to two dear brothers. For however long it lasted, she chose to enjoy it.

She stood and reached back around to untie the ribbons of her dress. After a fruitless struggle, she knew she must seek Stephen's help. She cracked open the door and peeked into the family room and found him leaning against the fireplace, an expression of deep thought on his face. He had removed his uniform coat and boots and wore only his shirt and buff breeches.

"Stephen," she called out softly.

He jerked his head. "Anything amiss, Tessa?"

She hesitated, her cheeks growing hot. "I believe I need your help removing my dress. I mean...untying the ribbons."

He followed her into the bedroom and walked around behind her. She lifted up her hair, and he began unlacing the dress. His fingers grazed the small of her back, stealing her breath.

When he paused, she closed her eyes and wished that he might kiss her neck.

He cleared his throat and stepped away. She pressed the bodice against her breasts and hurried behind the screen in the corner of the room. She removed the dress and corset, leaving her wearing nothing but her shift.

"Umm. I forgot my nightgown. It was a gift from Mrs. Stanton. She draped it across the foot of the bed. Would you hand it to me?"

He mumbled something she couldn't make out, and then she caught the gown as it glided over the top of the screen.

She brushed her fingertips across the fabric, enjoying the cool, diaphanous texture so new to her. Her stomach trembling, she squared her shoulders and stepped from around the screen. She took a ribbon from the vanity and tied it around her hair with hands that shook so badly, she almost caught a finger in the bow. She draped her hair across one shoulder and over her chest and faced Stephen, who still had not said one word, but stared at her with a grim expression. He stood perfectly still except for the twitching muscle below his temple. His eyes were glowing pools of golden-brown.

Suddenly overcome with shyness, she rushed over to the

bed and slid under the covers. She pushed a pillow behind her and sat up with her back pressed against the headboard.

Stephen grabbed a pillow and pulled a blanket from the end of the bed. "I'll bid you goodnight, then."

"You do not plan to sleep here?"

He swallowed so hard, his Adam's apple bobbed. "I thought it best to sleep in the other room."

"On the floor? Surely not. I know you are as tired as I and need a comfortable place to rest."

Stephen chuckled. "I have slept in many uncomfortable situations...on cold, wet mud and sandy beaches without a blanket and with Knight's saddle for a pillow."

Tessa pulled back the covers from the other side of the bed and patted the mattress, inviting him to join her. "Please, I insist. I would not get rest myself worrying about you."

He glanced up at the ceiling for a moment. "If you insist."

He replaced the pillow and blanket and stepped away to remove his breeches, allowing his shirt to billow around his knees.

He wore nothing underneath the shirt, and Tessa could not drag her gaze away from him. Why had she insisted? She played with fire, but she wanted him close.

He quickly slipped into the bed, stuffed the pillow behind his head, and lay on his back with the covers pulled up to his chin.

Tessa breathed in the pleasant aroma of bay leaves and limes that wafted across the bed.

Stephen was so tall, his feet pushed out from under the covers and hung over the edge of the mattress. Tessa could not stifle a giggle.

"May I know what's so amusing?"

"It's your feet, Stephen. You are much too tall for this bed." She pressed fingers to her mouth.

He chuckled. "It's a good thing there are no mosquitos around." He sat up and scooted his back against the headboard.

Tessa laughed out loud until the covers slipped, exposing his chest hair beneath his open collar.

Shaken, she picked up a tress of her hair and wound it around her fingers. "It was an amazing day, was it not?"

"It's certainly one I'll never forget."

"Nor I."

Sitting up in bed, propped by pillows, and sharing laughter and their thoughts of the day gave Tessa a glimpse of what life could be like as a married couple.

It was something she desired, and she desired it with Stephen. But would he love her when their charade was over? Enough to continue their marriage?

They remained quiet for a while, and Tessa's body relaxed and sank into the mattress. Her eyelids grew heavy, but she fought against them, not wanting this special time to end.

Stephen picked up a Bible from the nightstand and removed a white feather from the binding crease. "It seems Mrs. Stanton has marked a place she wishes us to read."

"She is the most thoughtful of women." Tessa yawned and closed her eyes. "What does it say?"

～

Stephen scrolled his finger down the page to a small pencil mark. "It's Ecclesiastes 4:9. 'Two are better than one, because they have a good return for their labor. If either of them falls down, one can help the other up.'"

He stopped reading to consider the times he and Tessa had buffered one another. How comforting it would be to have a permanent helpmate.

He continued reading aloud. "'But pity anyone who falls

and has no one to help them up. Also, if two lie down together, they will keep warm. But how can one keep warm alone?'"

Thoughts of keeping Tessa warm stirred his blood.

"Mrs. Stanton *is* the most thoughtful of women, indeed." He closed the book and returned it to the nightstand. "Tessa—"

With her back against the headboard, her head lolled to the side. She had fallen into a deep sleep.

He rolled onto his side and feasted his eyes upon her. Her golden hair splayed across her pillow, and her lips parted slightly as she breathed. Her eyelashes, a shade darker than her hair, feathered against her peach-colored cheeks. How incredibly beautiful and desirable she was. He could reach out right now and make her his.

Though she tried to hide it, she had revealed in countless ways her attraction for him. But she craved the deep, enduring love of a soulmate...the kind her mother and father shared. He desired to give her that depth of love. Should he tell her and face her possible rejection? He'd never shown cowardice before, so why did he hesitate now?

He scooped her up and laid her flat. He lifted her head and rested it on her pillow and pulled the covers up under her chin. She sighed softly, and her eyelids fluttered, but she nestled under the covers and slept soundly. He turned onto his side, hugging the edge of the bed, and extinguished the lantern.

He awoke early. Though the bedroom had no windows, the familiar sounds of clinking metal and cadenced footsteps as the soldiers and horses marched out of the compound told him it was dawn.

Tessa had not moved a muscle all night except to lay her hand across his stomach. He gently lifted it and tucked it under the covers. He slid out of bed, donned his breeches, and tiptoed out of the room.

The night had been more restful than he'd anticipated. Lying beside one of the most alluring women he had ever known should have kept him awake, but the rhythmic sound of her breathing had lulled him to sleep.

In the front room, he tripped over Tessa's rucksack that lay on its side next to a wingback chair. A number of her sketches spilled out onto the floor. He gathered them up and would have put them away, but several caught his eye. Many of the drawings were of travelers on the wagon train.

In one, the young newlyweds sat together on their wagon seat, their expressions full of adoration. Another pictured the Kerns, a German couple, walking beside their herd of goats. Tessa had depicted the two baby goats especially as so soft and cuddly and playful, Stephen had to touch them. Had Sally been their mother? The one of Mr. Tucker, a cobbler traveling alone, made him chuckle. The man sat on a stump, one leg crossed over the other. He had shoved his glasses up onto his forehead and was poking out his bottom lip, deeply concentrating on sewing the sole of a boot. Dozens of her drawings captured the soul and character of her subjects...each a masterpiece.

Those clear blue eyes of hers registered more than he realized.

When had she had time to create them? He thought back to their first week together on the wagon train and remembered waking up in the middle of the night and seeing a candle glowing in her wagon. The blue smudges underneath her eyes that, at the time, he thought were from fatigue had really been caused by sleeplessness. Over the past week, often at night after supper, she would sit quietly with a pencil or pen or charcoal scratching across the surface of her sketch paper. She had dated and signed them. Some of them she had rendered recently. How had she managed to depict each person with such detail without them sitting for her?

What a remarkable memory.

He smiled. His wife was brilliant. No, she was a genius. A treasure.

He returned the sketches to the rucksack and spent time contemplating what lay ahead in Camden. Would they head straight for the horse farm? Should he find accommodations for Tessa, and then he and his brothers go to the farm? How soon after their arrival would they initiate the divorce proceedings? Would he want a divorce? Would she?

He paced up and down in front of the fireplace until a tap sounded on the front door. He opened it to Francis, who balanced a tray laden with eggs and bacon, jam and biscuits. Adam followed carrying a teapot wrapped in quilted towels.

"Good morning." Adam's expression glowed with enthusiasm.

Stephen put his finger to his lips. "Shh. Tessa is still asleep."

The door to the bedroom opened, and Tessa stepped into the room. "No, I'm quite awake."

The light blue of her dress complemented her lively eyes and her slightly tanned skin. The bodice that tied in the front emphasized her slim waist. She had tucked her glorious hair under a mobcap.

She was as pretty as one of her pictures.

"You look rested." Stephen's tepid response did not match the tightness in his chest.

Her cheeks flushed, and she fingered the folds of her petticoats. "I slept surprisingly well."

"Come and sit, Tessa," Francis invited and seated her at the table. "Mrs. Stanton gave strict orders that you and Stephen eat while it's warm."

"I am to pour." Adam proceeded to pour tea through a strainer he had placed onto one of the cups. "Cream and sugar, Mrs. Griffith?"

Tessa's eyes lit. "Both, please. And may I say it's lovely to be called by my new name?"

Stephen tucked into the meal and resisted the urge to wipe away the tiny bit of jam at the corner of Tessa's mouth.

Adam sat at the table with them, and his eyes never left the food.

Francis plopped down in the wingback chair and draped his leg over one of the arms. "You should have seen the soldiers this morning. I especially liked the fife and drum."

Adam propped his elbows on the table. "Yes. The soldiers were grand. Lined up in the straightest of rows, their musket bayonets razor sharp."

Tessa put down her teacup. "You'd like to be a soldier, Adam?"

Stephen perked up. Why was she asking that?

Adam's eyes brightened. "Yes. I believe I would like that very much."

Stephen looked from Tessa to Adam and back again. They had talked about this.

"What of school?" Stephen asked.

"I want to be a soldier, just like you."

How could he resist the entreaty on his little brother's face?

"Maybe you could do both. But it's a subject we'll consider at another time." Stephen caught the wink Tessa sent Adam's way.

When they had finished eating, Adam kept staring at the last biscuit remaining on the servicing dish.

"You may have it," Tessa said with a smile. "And there's a bit of jam left too."

She was already aware of the boys and their needs. They missed their mother and could use some female attention. Another reason to remain married?

Stephen sat back in his chair. "While we're together, I want to hear your thoughts about how soon you'd like to get back onto the trail."

"I'm for leaving sooner than later," Francis offered.

Adam swallowed the biscuit and licked the jam from his upper lip. "I agree."

"What say you, Stephen?" Francis swung his leg back over the chair arm and sat up.

"You know me. I like a routine...a schedule. I'm ready to leave in a moment's notice."

Besides, he would rather lie on a bed of nails than spend one more night sleeping next to Tessa without touching her.

"Tessa?" he asked.

"I do worry a bit about what awaits us in Camden, but there's no warrant in postponing. I will concur with your decision." Tessa looked away.

Was she worried that reaching Camden meant divorce?

Stephen rose and stood behind his chair, curling his hands around the spindles. "It's settled. I don't see why we can't leave today. The wagon is almost completely packed. I arranged for some provisions with the mess steward, including a bag of oats for Knight. We'll need to stop by the stream outside the fort and fill our water barrels."

Their preparations went so smoothly, they were packed and ready to leave at noon.

Mrs. Stanton, who stood next to Tessa, handed a basket to Adam perched on the wagon seat. "It's a little something to eat. Ham and biscuits, jam, cake, and strawberries."

Adam's eyebrows shot up, and he waggled them at Francis.

Tessa gulped. "You've done so much for us already, Katherine. I'm so thrilled about the petticoats and the lovely shawl you gave me."

Mrs. Stanton kissed Tessa's forehead. "I would love to do more. You are very special to me now, my dear. It's almost like having a daughter."

For Stephen, their departure meant leaving behind the relative safety of the fort. Even more, he regretted the emotional farewell between Tessa and Mrs. Stanton. Their tears mingled as they hugged and pressed their cheeks together.

Outside, on the road leading from the fort, he twisted

around on Knight to catch Mrs. Stanton inside the gateway waving goodbye with her lace handkerchief, and Tessa stretching out over the edge of the seat waving back.

Worrying over his wife's reactions. He was well and truly a married man, though in name only.

He straightened in the saddle and mulled over the Bible verse he had read on their wedding night. *Two are better than one. If either of them falls down, one can help the other up.* He could easily fulfill that promise. But what of the words, *Also, if two lie down together, they will keep warm*? Could he lie beside her again, close enough to keep her warm, and still leave the option open for her to dissolve their union? With more questions than answers roiling around in his head, he prodded Knight with his knees and led their way south.

CHAPTER 16

*T*essa and Francis sat on either side of Adam as he drove the wagon over an increasingly rough and rocky section of the trail. They slammed into a huge hole, bouncing her up from the seat. She would have been tossed off if Francis hadn't reached around Adam and grabbed her arm.

She tittered and then rearranged her rumpled skirts and straightened her hat. "Thank you, Francis."

"I think you may have missed a rut, Adam." Francis rubbed his backside. "You want to go back and get it?"

"Ha. Very funny. I'm doing the best I can." Adam wrapped the reins tighter around his hands. "Do we even know where we are?" he yelled to Stephen, who rode farther up the trail.

Stephen halted and waited for the wagon to catch up. "We're only two days out from Fort Hampton, so we should be a couple of weeks away from the North Carolina colony. I showed you on a map in Colonel Stanton's office the other evening." He scanned the woods around them. "Look around us and tell me, is there anything different from where we've come from?"

Tessa, who had been soaking up the changes in the terrain, answered first. "We passed by many enticing prospects—meandering rivers, grassy meadows, the leathery deep-green leaves of mountain laurel shrubs. And more and more cedar trees. It would take a thousand hues of green for me to recreate them."

Stephen grinned. "Spoken like a true artist."

Flattered, Tessa returned his smile.

"Come on, fellows, what say you?" Stephen pulled his right foot from the stirrup and leaned his leg across Knight's neck.

The muscles in his thigh bulged, and Tessa struggled to put her attention elsewhere.

"There are more and more huge granite rocks, and the trail sure is rougher. More up and down," said Adam.

"Good. And you, Francis?"

Francis scratched his head. "The last stream we filled our barrels with...the water was freezing cold."

Stephen nodded. "Good observations. All those things let us know we have reached the foothills of the Blue Ridge Mountains. The air will get thinner during the day, and we, as well as our horses, may have difficulty breathing. The nights will be cooler too." He moved his foot back into the stirrup. "Let's move along. We've much more trail to cover."

When Stephen returned to his place yards ahead of the wagon, Francis pulled his harmonica from his waistcoat pocket and started playing a tune.

Tessa clapped her hands. "I know this one."

> Baa, baa, black sheep,
> Have you any wool?
> Yes sir, yes sir,
> Three bags full.

Adam sang the second verse along with her.

> One for the master,
> One for the dame,

And one for the little boy
Who lives down the lane.

Adam's voice broke several times during the song, sliding from tenor to soprano and back again. Stephen twisted around in his saddle and made eye contact with Tessa, who fought to keep a straight face. Just as they finished singing, a howl reverberated through the woods.

"That wolf is either singing along or he is protesting your singing voice, Adam," Stephen called over his shoulder.

Francis was the first to laugh, followed by Tessa and Stephen, and finally Adam.

They had made a wonderful family memory.

They rode about an hour farther, then stopped long enough to eat lunch and rest the horses. Back on the trail, Tessa found herself once again enraptured by the magnificent prospects that surrounded her.

Though portraits were her forte, she had experimented with landscapes and had even painted the backgrounds her father had required for clients who desired to be portrayed in exotic settings. The many canvases stored in a crate in the wagon included her illustrations of an English country garden, an Italian palazzo, and a Spanish castillo. One very eccentric man had wanted his portrait painted depicting him as a Viking. The memory of her father rolling his eyes when informed of his client's wishes gave her spirits a lift.

While repacking the wagon that morning, Tessa had discovered a letter to her father from the man they'd agreed to meet in Camden—Martin Crosswell. Would he want to work with her? Would he think her work good enough?

Stop worrying. God will provide.

She turned her attention to Stephen, who still rode point guard for the wagon. Her love for him deepened with each passing hour since she had acknowledged it to herself. His every expression, every movement, the timbre of his voice, his laughter with the boys, his endearing affection for Knight, all brightened her life just as a stroke of white brushed over the darkest shadows of a painting brought light and balance and new life.

The memory of their wedding night tingled her spine. She had wanted more. Had he?

Stephen turned around and came alongside the wagon, removed his hat, and wiped his brow on his shirtsleeve. His sweat-drenched hair flattened against the crown of his head, while tendrils curled around his ears and neck. Another man might look unkempt, but Tessa found him endearing.

"I've decided to make camp early. It will give me a chance to show each of you how to fire a musket."

"I say," Francis shouted his approval.

Adam whooped.

Tessa managed to refrain from clutching her hand to her throat. "I am included?"

He stared at her with an expression more serious than he had ever shown. "Yes, Tessa. You must learn to defend yourself." He glanced at his brothers. "I've been remiss in not teaching you sooner, but will make up for it. Especially in light of what we've experienced and that we are a lone, vulnerable wagon now."

Vulnerable. What a disturbing word. Would knowing how to use a firearm make her feel less so? Doubtful.

He pointed toward a break in the trees. "There's a spot up ahead. Adam...you all right to guide the horses off the road?"

"Certainly. Lead the way." Adam slapped the reins, urging the team forward.

They set up camp and ate a light supper of leftover beef stew and biscuits. The boys gobbled their food while Tessa barely nibbled, trying not to upset her nervous stomach any more than it already was.

She and the boys followed Stephen to a clearing where he set up targets he had fashioned out of grain sacks. He laid out two muskets and two pistols.

"Boys, I know you're excited, but you must realize…these are deadly weapons, not toys. Safety is a primary concern. Right now, I'm going to teach you how to handle, load, and fire them. A lesson on how to clean them will come another time."

In the short period she had known them, the boys had adapted to their surroundings as if they had lived in the wilderness all their lives. The same held true of loading a weapon. They both caught on quickly as Stephen took time with them and showed patience.

A natural leader, he inspired confidence. His controlling manner could have rankled, but he tempered it, especially treating Tessa gently and with kindness.

"Aim small, miss small," he instructed, straightening the barrel of the musket Francis braced against his shoulder.

When Francis finally fired the round, the deafening roar caused Tessa to hunch her shoulders and clasp her hands over her ears. Stephen watched her closely, a grim expression on his face. When she tried to pick up the musket, his frown grew more intense.

"It's almost as tall as she, Stephen. And much too heavy," Francis observed, holding a musket in the crook of his elbow.

"I can see that. Here, Tessa. This may suit better." He picked up one of the flintlock pistols and handed it to her.

She groaned as the weight of it felt as if it might break her arm.

"That won't do either. You do have the tiniest of wrists." Stephen laid the pistol back on the ground. "I know. Give me a moment."

He ran to the wagon and returned a few minutes later holding up a strange triangular leather object. "It's a katar dagger."

He pulled the knife from its sheath and handed it to her. Palm-sized, the dagger had an *H*-shaped handle and a four-inch blade.

"Whoa," Adam exclaimed. "I thought my knife was special."

Stephen rubbed his thumb over the blade. "Many Indian princes and noblemen carry these daggers. Some use them to hunt tigers, as proof of their courage."

Tessa had knowledge of people and art, but he had so much more experience of the world. Could she truly match a man like that?

He curled his fingers through the top of the knife handle and swept his hand down. "It's for plunging, not pointing."

Tessa took the dagger, slid it into its sheath, and put it in the under-pocket of her petticoats. "I thank you, Stephen, but I cannot imagine that I will ever have need of it."

"People do many things when their life or the life of someone they love is threatened."

He stared into her eyes so intensely, she glanced away at their small armory. "I fear I won't be much use if it comes to it."

His lips softened. "Don't despair. I'll teach you how to make cartridges, which is an extremely valuable skill."

The boys left them, Adam to practice throwing his knife and Francis to gather the muskets and pistols and take down the targets.

Stephen led Tessa to a flat boulder near the edge of a cliff overlooking a valley far below. A silver-blue ribbon, a river threaded its way through stands of trees of every sort and color. Thick patches of wildflowers spread across the riverbanks as a lush blanket.

"How lovely," Tessa exclaimed, once again longing for her paints and brushes.

"Very." Stephen regarded her and not the prospect.

He sat beside her and pulled some objects from the leather pouch suspended around his chest next to a powder horn.

"Now, to the lesson. This is a lead ball...about the size of a marble. It goes in the bottom of the piece of paper. Then comes the black powder." He popped the top off the horn and poured powder into the paper. "You keep it all together by twisting the paper into a tail."

Tessa examined the cartridge. "I can do this."

"Of course you can." He handed her the powder horn.

"Paper, lead ball, black powder, and twist the paper." Tessa repeated the process and held out the finished product.

"Well done for your first try. You'll soon learn that the finer the paper, the truer the aim. Some men use silk cloth for the best results."

His praise warmed her heart. "I'll practice really hard. I want to do my part."

Francis joined them, laid the firearms and targets on the ground, and sat beside Tessa.

"Where's Adam going?" Stephen watched his younger brother hurry toward the campfire.

"Said he was ready for bed."

"That's odd, don't you think?" Tessa asked. "Adam never voluntarily beds down early."

Francis scooped up the guns and targets and headed for the wagon.

Stephen held out his hand to Tessa. "It's time we went back ourselves. The sun will be down soon."

Tessa took his hand and allowed him to assist her up from the rock. She didn't want to let go. Would she be forced to, just when she grew accustomed to his touch?

CHAPTER 17

essa awoke before dawn the next morning as the sun started to burn away the pale blue-gray mist that hovered in the forest like a shroud. Lingering on his pallet, Francis yawned and stretched. He poked Adam with his foot, but his brother remained still. Stephen and Tessa leaned against the wagon wheel and observed the stars disappear behind pink and orange veils of light.

Stephen turned toward her. "Will you come with me, Tessa?"

What could he want? With a tinge of eagerness, she accompanied him to the overlook, where she sat on a granite shelf that jutted out over the cliff.

He crouched in front of her, his eyes level with hers. His searching countenance made her pulse quicken.

"I have something I want to say—"

"Stephen! Tessa! Come quickly," Francis yelled, racing across the clearing. "There's something terribly wrong with Adam."

They all ran to the pallet where Adam lay near the campfire.

Francis, his face a ghostly white, spoke through trembling lips. "I tried to get him up, but he hasn't the strength. And... and...he's trying to talk but isn't making any sense."

Stephen dropped to his knees and gently shook his brother. "Adam? Adam? Can you hear me?"

Tessa knelt beside him as Adam stared at them, dazed. "Let's check his arms and legs for rashes or bites. Snake...bug."

When she pushed up his right sleeve and spotted the bloody bandage crudely wrapped around his forearm, she gasped. She pulled the torn bits of cloth away and exposed a three-inch-long gash in the skin now turned a hot, ugly yellow-ish-red.

Stephen's spine stiffened. "It's a knife wound. I've seen it many times before."

"Why didn't he say something?" Tessa ran her fingers down Adam's arm to soothe him.

"He must have injured himself aiming for the targets and thought you would take the knife away from him," Francis whispered.

"It's inflamed." Stephen's tone was solemn. His pupils dilated and his hand shook.

"He will be well. Won't he?" Francis dropped onto one knee, touching Adam's leg.

"Francis, fetch my medicine kit from the wagon. It's a cedar chest about this big." Tessa indicated the size with her hands.

When Francis handed her the kit, Tessa opened the lid and sorted through various-sized cork-topped pots and vials. "Oh, dear. I hadn't realized my supplies had depleted so much. I do have a little ginger. That's supposed to help against inflammation."

Stephen gulped and balled up his fists. "Honey? Do you have honey? On the battlefields, I saw many surgeons use it to heal infections from cuts, bullet wounds, and amputations."

"There's no honey." Tessa pursed her bottom lip. "But did I

not hear someone at the fort say there would be a trading post down the trail? Should we turn back to the fort or go ahead?"

Stephen clasped her shoulders and kissed her cheek. "The trading post is closer, and they might have what we need."

Tessa touched her cheek where his lips had touched. His small gesture made her heartbeat skip.

She grabbed a handful of covers. "I'll make a pallet and ride in back with him."

Francis opened the backboard and helped her into the wagon, where she spread the covers on the narrow open aisle between the stacks of chests and crates. Stephen scooped up Adam, and once they had him settled, Tessa climbed back down and helped gather their belongings that Stephen shoved into the back corners under the canvas. Tessa threw her rucksack over her shoulder and had just bounced up and down trying to reach the spring step when Stephen picked her up by the waist and placed her on the backboard. His face was pale, and deep worry lines furrowed his brow.

Dejection—an unfamiliar emotion for him. She could not bear to see him this way.

She could not resist cupping his cheek with her hand. "He'll get well. How could he not with so much love surrounding him?"

He pressed his hand to hers and then turned away. "Francis, I'll get Knight. You're in charge of the wagon."

Tessa tucked the coverlet under Adam's chin and felt his forehead. As Stephen headed toward Knight, she called out to him, "Adam has a fever. I'll need a bucket of water from the stream to cool him off."

Stephen stopped walking and his shoulders drooped.

Lord, we need your help.

Stephen returned with the water, and mounted on Knight, he stared into the wagon and watched Tessa sponge Adam's trembling body.

She wrung a cloth and draped it across Adam's forehead. "It's helping."

"I'm not sure what I would do without you, Tessa."

Did he have any idea what his words meant to her?

She pulled the covers up around Adam's neck. "I think we can leave now."

They headed out of the clearing and back onto the trail. The sun had already set by the time they reached the trading post and tavern, and Tessa could not have been more relieved. The inflammation had spread streaks of red up to Adam's elbow, and chills shook him from head to toe.

Francis helped her from the wagon and ran to attach Knight's reins to a tethering line in the front yard of the trading post. "Must be quite a crowd here. There's more than twenty horses."

Stephen gathered Adam into his arms, and they hurried inside the sprawling wooden building. The crowd of men seated at tables and standing at the bar immediately went silent and stared.

The barmaid behind the counter stopped running a cloth around a tankard. Her features were unusual and quite beautiful. Her unruly ebony curls framed her heart-shaped face and tumbled across her shoulders and down her back. Her eyes shone a light purple—a color so uncommon, Tessa tried to think what shades she would need to mix to paint them. The untied bodice of her yellow dress exposed the top of her generous bosom.

Where had Tessa seen the sunflower pattern of the barmaid's dress?

Stephen placed Adam in a chair near the entrance, and Francis propped him against his side.

"My brother has an infected wound," Stephen said to the barmaid. "We need alcohol, honey, and bandages. Can you help us? I will pay whatever you say."

Tessa took her first long look at the men, who mumbled among themselves. They huddled in the shadows. Their filthy, greasy clothing were those of frontiersmen—fringed leggings, trade shirts, boots or moccasins. But not the first one had bathed in quite a while.

Something was wrong. The presence of evil ran chills down Tessa's arms.

The woman cackled. "You've come to the right place. This lot always has some wound or other ailment." She pointed to Tessa. "Your missus?"

Stephen pulled off his hat. "I beg your pardon. I'm Stephen Griffith, and this is my wife and my two brothers."

"I'm Violet." She sauntered to the end of the counter closest to Tessa and lifted the board separating her from the room. "Come with me, Mrs. Griffith."

Tessa exchanged glances with Stephen, who nodded. She followed the woman along the path between the counter and the lines of tankards, liquor bottles, kegs, and ale barrels. With each step, her shoes stuck to the floor. She kept her eyes straight ahead, avoiding what might be scattered on the planks.

When they reached the end of the counter, one of the men sidled close to Tessa. A leer distorted his face, and he smelled so awful, she was hard-pressed not to hold her nose. Instead, her hand went straight to her waist and the reassuring feel of the knife under her petticoats.

The woman pressed her hand against the man's chest and shoved so hard he almost fell. "Out of my way, Tom."

"Just takin' a gander, Violet." He grinned at Tessa, exposing rows of rotten teeth.

"Go sit down. I'll bring you some ale in a minute." Violet waved Tessa toward a room lined with mostly empty shelves. "We don't do much business here."

Tessa followed her to a cabinet loaded with bottles, pots,

and rolled-up bandages. She discovered a jar with the label *Honey.* "Thank the good Lord. It's just what we need."

Violet crept up close to her and whispered, "Take what you need and get away from here as fast as you can. It's not safe for you and your family."

Tessa's back muscles stiffened. She lowered her head and whispered back, "Thank you. My husband will pay and then we will do as you say."

"Fine. But hurry."

Violet shoved bandages, honey, and several vials into Tessa's rucksack and shepherded her back into the tavern, but the sounds of shouting and the blows of fists brought them to a halt. Near the tavern door, a man lifted Francis up into the air and slammed him down onto the table where Adam had been sitting.

Tessa screamed in horror.

Adam lay in a daze underneath the table where Francis now also sprawled, unconscious. At the foot of the bar, Stephen grappled with three men who wrestled him to the floor, shoved him over onto his stomach, and bound his hands behind him.

"No!" Tessa shrieked, but when she tried to run to him, Violet grabbed her arm, knocking her mobcap to the floor.

Violet pushed Tessa behind her. "Don't interfere. You'll make it worse."

The brawl ended in minutes. The men heaved Stephen to a standing position. The one who had thrown Francis picked him up and shook him awake. Francis vomited on the man's boot, and the man growled and scuffed him on the back of his head.

"What's happening?" Violet yelled.

Tom pointed to Francis. "These people...they was on the wagon train...survived somehow. That one, there, recognized my carved powder horn. Said he knows it belonged to the wagon master. Wanted to know how I came by it. It was only a matter of time afore they figured out what we done. That it was us and not Indians."

"Shut up, you fool!" someone ordered.

A tall, lanky man stretched himself up from one of the chairs. His light-blond hair was pulled into a queue elegantly tied with a black satin ribbon. Despite the sweltering temperature, he wore a blue velvet waistcoat. Like a cat with a mouse, he sauntered his way across the floor to Stephen. Some of the men made way while others slunk back into the shadows.

Tessa trembled.

I am in the presence of evil. Lord, protect us.

Blood flowed down Stephen's scalp and nose, dripped across his lips and chin, and dribbled onto his shirt. Though battered, he stiffened his spine when the man halted inches away.

"May I introduce myself? I am Jared, the leader of this fine band of men." He spoke with a slight French accent. He bowed low and swept his arm out in an exaggerated imitation of a courtier.

Several of the men chortled and made mock bows to one another.

"So, Mr. Griffith, you and your family pose a problem for me and my men. You know our little secret. Yes? What shall I do with you?"

"Kill the men and give us the woman," someone called out.

Stephen thrashed around, receiving a punch in the stomach for his efforts. In a panic, Tessa tried to go to him, but someone grabbed her rucksack. It slipped off her shoulder and skittered across the floor, spilling out the contents.

Jared picked up the papers, pulled others from the rucksack, and spread them across the bar. "You did these?" he asked, not taking his eyes from the sketches.

"I did," Tessa said softly.

He displayed a couple of the pictures to the men. "We have

a master artist among us." He motioned to Violet. "Come, my dove. Are they not marvelous?"

Violet skirted by Tessa and joined Jared, who wrapped his arm around her waist. She scanned the drawings and looked back and forth from them to Tessa. "Impressive."

Jared swung around to give his full attention to Tessa, who hooded her eyes and stared at the worn, filthy floor planks.

"I have an idea. A proposition of sorts. Mrs. Griffith, would you be willing to paint a portrait of my Violet?" He pulled Violet closer. "I would pay you handsomely."

Violet's expression remained blank.

"I would. That thought crossed my mind the moment I saw her. She would make a lovely study."

Someone guffawed. "A lovely study," he mimicked.

Tessa's stomach knotted. "But I have a proposition of my own. If you like the portrait, do not pay me with money, but with freedom for me and my family."

Jared threw back his head and laughed out loud. "Ha! You dare to make a counter proposal!"

Tessa looked directly at him for the first time. His visage was not as sinister or debauched as she had expected. Quite the opposite. Altogether, his broad forehead, strong Greek nose, angled cheekbones, and symmetrical lips made him one of the handsomest men she had ever met.

He struck a pose and pretended to contemplate her offer. "If I like it, you say?" He stuck out his hand. "'Tis a good bargain."

Tessa proffered her hand to shake, but he clasped it and bowed over it, bringing his face inches from hers. His blue eyes were a shade darker than her own.

A person could be consumed by them.

He grinned. "I promise, sweet lady, despite what you might think, I am a man of my word. But I sense you feel as if you have made a deal with the devil. *Oui?*" he whispered.

I do. But greater is He that is in me than he that is in the world.

CHAPTER 18

*L*ate in the evening, locked inside a large bare room in the tavern, Tessa, Stephen, and Francis huddled together praying while Adam slept fitfully on a cot in the corner. Keys rattled, and despite his hands being tied, Stephen placed himself between Tessa and the entrance.

"It's me." Violet pushed open the door and entered the room carrying a heavily laden tray. "I've brought food and water and medicine. I also brought your artwork, Tessa."

Tessa squeezed the treasured bag to her chest. "Thank you, Violet. I wasn't sure I'd ever see it again."

Tom lumbered into the room hauling two buckets so full of water, he sloshed it across the floor.

"Put them over there, Tom." Violet pointed to a bench jutting out from the wall across from Adam's cot. "Before you go, untie Mr. Griffith. And remember the orders...no one is to be hurt in any way."

"Yeh, yeh," Tom mumbled. He grabbed Stephen's bound hands and sawed the rope loose with his knife. "There, see? Didn't hurt him a bit." He left the room to stand outside the door.

Stephen flexed his fingers and massaged the red streaks on his wrists. He took the tankard Violet held out to him.

"This here is ground cinchona bark tea to help bring down the fever. Start spooning it now and keep going till it's gone," Violet instructed. "It's a little bitter, so I added sugar."

Stephen waited for Francis to hop onto the cot behind Adam and prop his back against him. At first, Adam resisted the medication, turning his head away and clamping his lips together.

Stephen pressed the spoon against Adam's lips but succeeded only in dribbling most of it down his brother's chin, "Please. Drink this, Adam. It will make you feel better."

"Let me." Violet took Stephen's place. "You need tending to yourself."

Stephen gingerly touched the gash at his hairline and grimaced. The blood from that and from his battered nose had already dried into crusty streaks down his face and neck.

Tessa tore off a piece of bandage and dipped it into one of the buckets. "Come, Stephen, sit on the bench."

He sat down, and she stood between his knees gingerly wiping away the caked blood. He looked up at her with eyes filled with sadness.

"I'm sorry, Tessa."

Frowning, she stood back. "For what?"

"For not protecting you."

She so desired to kiss his forehead and run her fingers through his hair.

Instead, she pushed a tendril of his hair behind his ear. "There were dozens of them. No one could have withstood them. I'm thankful you weren't hurt any worse than you are."

Francis gasped. "It's all my fault. If I hadn't said anything about the powder horn..." He started to cry.

Violet scoffed. "None of that. What's done is done. Hold

your brother steady." She peeked over her shoulder at the door. "Our problem now is how we are going to get you out of here."

A tiny ray of hope burst alive in Tessa's heart. "You will help us?"

"I'll do my best. Hand me the pot with the honey. You might put some honey on Stephen's wound too."

When Violet finished using the honey, Tessa spread some on Stephen's cuts and secured a bandage around his forehead. Again, the desire to hug him and kiss the top of his head almost overwhelmed her, but she moved away.

"I'll be right back." Violet put down the tankard and spoon, walked out the door, and returned minutes later with a lantern and blankets. "Try and rest. I'll start working on a plan," she whispered.

She left and Tom slammed the door. The sound of the key locking jarred Tessa, and she slid to the floor, shaking uncontrollably.

"Tessa!" Stephen dropped down beside her.

"What have I done? Making a bargain with such an evil man?" She clasped Stephen's forearms. "He is so evil, it frightens me. Can I really paint a portrait well enough to suit him? Can such a monster be trusted to keep his side of the bargain?"

Stephen cradled her on his lap. "It's apparent that Violet doesn't think so. And also why she's going ahead with an escape plan." He pulled her hands away from her face. "Are you able to go along with the bargain until she figures something out? I know we're asking a great deal, but playing along with Jared will give us time to plan and ready ourselves."

Francis joined them. "You can do this, Tessa. You're a wonderful painter and so brave to have faced up to that man."

Stephen helped Tessa to her feet. "Francis, spread the covers on the floor next to the cot. Though Adam seems to be responding to the medicine, I'll keep watch on him for a while. I'll turn the lantern down."

A wave of fatigue rolled through Tessa's body, and her knees trembled. She lay on her back on the pallet between Stephen and Francis and folded an arm across her eyes. She reached out her other arm, seeking Stephen's hand, and entwined her fingers in his.

Lord, I'm simply too tired to pray. You know what's on my heart.

CHAPTER 19

*T*essa sat with Violet at one of the tables in the tavern drinking a strong brew that Violet called coffee but tasted of boiled pine bark. None of the men frequented the bar in the early morning, but the smell of stale beer, tobacco, and body odor permeated the air.

Tessa had left Stephen and the boys after Violet brought them breakfast. Though imprisoned, they had food and water and relative peace. Adam had improved much overnight, but his body still fought the infection, and his health teetered in the balance.

Violet sipped her coffee. "How is this portrait going to happen?"

"All artists are different. It's my way to talk with my subjects. Become acquainted and get a feeling for their character. Then I make sketches from different angles and poses until I find one that reaches out to me."

Tessa positioned her sketchpad and a pencil on the table in front of her. She studied Violet, whose appearance had altered amazingly from the night before. She had gathered her massive ebony curls and secured them on top of her head, allowing long strands to flow loosely along the sides of her face. Two rows of lace embellished the scooped neck and puffed sleeves of her shift. Over the undergarment, she wore a leather vest cinched tight, accentuating her tiny waist. Men's breeches and a pair of knee-high boots completed her costume.

A sensual woman secure in her femininity enough to wear a man's clothing. I could not be so bold.

Overcome with the familiar urge to create, Tessa picked up her pencil and began moving it across the paper. The two of them remained silent while she completed a series of four sketches so quickly she surprised herself.

Violet held up one of them. "This is how you see me?"

"Yes."

"You have made me beautiful."

The astonishment on her face was even more puzzling than her words. Did she not realize how lovely she was?

Tessa retrieved her fan from her rucksack and fluttered her face with it. "Violet, is it permitted for us to go outside? It's stifling in here."

"Certainly. Many of the men left last night and won't return for a day or two. One never knows." She carried their mugs to the bar. "The rest of the lazy louts won't crawl out of their beds till after noon. They wouldn't dare bother me, anyway."

Outside, Tessa breathed deeply and reveled in the fresh morning air. They walked toward a fallen log at the edge of the forest, where a mist still lingered. A mountain laurel bush caught her attention, and she wandered over to it and plucked one of the blossoms.

"They look like fine china," she said, holding the blossom to her nose. "It smells like grapes."

"Be careful. The nectar can cause a rash. Many beautiful things in the wilderness have an ugly side."

Like Jared.

She tucked the flower into her rucksack and sat on the log

beside Violet, who picked up a stick and started scribbling in the sand.

"Tell me something about yourself, Violet. Your growing up...your family."

Violet stared off into the woods. "According to my mother, I can trace my family back to the Spaniards who explored the South Carolina colony two hundred years ago. I know that my grandfather was Spanish and that my grandmother was from Africa. I also know that they had an albino daughter...my mother."

"Oh! I remember once in England, my father was commissioned to paint a gentleman, and in his home was a painting of an albino boy. His pink eyes fascinated me so much, I kept going back to look at them."

"I don't remember my mother much except that she was regarded as a freak by some...even a witch. I never knew my father. So I have no family to speak of." She threw away the stick and crossed one ankle over the other. "A family took me in when my mother died. I have to say, though they fed and clothed me, they weren't kind. I ran away when I was fourteen. I worked in a tavern until Jared asked me to be with him. He has been my family ever since." She held up her hand. "And before you say it, I know he's an outlaw. He's done terrible things. But he has never once mistreated me. I love him."

Tessa could not understand the kind of love that allowed a person to overlook another's evil. For her, love flourished out of admiration, friendship, respect, and attraction. How could anyone ever admire a brute like Jared?

At that moment, he cantered on a stallion out of the woods, leading a group of his men.

Speak of the devil...

He rode up to them and tipped his hat. "Ladies. Taking in the air?"

Tessa could not look at him but stared at the toes of her shoes.

Violet laughed, walked over to him, and patted his horse's neck. "It seems that getting to know me is part of the process."

He slid down from his horse and motioned for one of the men to take it away. "Will I see progress soon?" he asked as he approached.

Spots of blood spattered the spurs on his boots. His poor horse. The man's cruelty knew no bounds. Anger welled up inside of Tessa, and she barely held her tongue. So far, Knight had not caught Jared's attention. What would happen when he did?

"Show him the sketches, Tessa."

Tessa reached into her bag and handed him the drawings, avoiding his touch as he took them from her.

"Hmm. I may have to ready myself to lose this proposition." He handed the sketches back. "Though I may win, after all."

Tessa tucked in her chin. Why did every word coming from his mouth have a double meaning?

"I'll have a fine portrait of my Violet to show for all my troubles." He curled his arm around Violet's waist and kissed her passionately.

Violet caressed his chest and gave him a gentle shove. "Come, Tessa. Let's go back inside."

When they entered the tavern, they were greeted by the rest of the men, who had finally climbed out of bed. Violet served them drinks while Tessa sat at her work table sharpening her graphite pencils with sandpaper.

Jared, holding a tankard of ale, sidled over to her. "How did you pass the night?"

Without glancing up, she said, "Adam's fever broke before dawn, and the honey is drawing out the inflammation."

"And Mr. Griffith?"

Did he truly care?

"He has recovered." She rested her pencil on her bottom lip.

"You have a fine man there. Fought like a lion for his family. I admire that."

Tessa recalled Stephen's bloody face and frowned.

Jared put down his tankard and eyed Violet as she served the men. "When will you start painting, and what can we do to make it happen? I'm eager to see who wins this contest."

"I need my trunk with my brushes and paints. I will also need a fresh canvas. That is, unless you want a special background. The samples of those are in a crate in our wagon."

Jared snapped his fingers and everyone grew silent. "Tom, take a couple of men to the Griffiths' wagon and let Mrs. Griffith show you what she needs."

Outside, Tessa climbed into the wagon and directed the men to the crate she wanted. She searched one of the chests and retrieved a clean mobcap, a brush, and a bar of soap and stuffed them into her rucksack. The men hauled the crate into the tavern along with the trunk containing her art supplies. They placed the trunk next to the bar and cracked open the crate, revealing several canvases that stood almost as tall as she. Per her instructions, the men arranged three of the canvasses on the counter behind the bar.

Tessa indicated each background in turn. "This is an English garden. This, an Italian palazzo, and this a Spanish castillo. Or, if you prefer, I can paint an original setting, but that would take much more time."

Jared raised an eyebrow. "I prefer an already prepared background."

A group of men stood in front of the bar, pointing to the canvases with expressions of awe. "*She* painted them?" one asked.

Jared and Violet walked back and forth viewing each rendering.

Violet lingered before the castillo. "Although this is Spanish, which is part of my heritage...this one"—she pointed to the garden—"appeals to me."

"The garden it is, then." Jared hugged her. "We shall title it *A Violet in an English Rose Garden*. And what a coincidence that my name in the Bible means *rose*. But I doubt I'll live nine hundred years."

A devil who knew the Bible? Beware.

One of the men guffawed, and Jared threw him a scowl that verged on lethal, giving Tessa a terrifying glimpse of his character without his mask.

In that moment, she recalled why the distinct pattern of the yellow dress Violet wore the first time they met seemed familiar. It had belonged to one of the women on the wagon train.

Underneath the elegant manners, handsome appearance, and affability dwelt a monster who had committed murder... including the murder of her father.

She mentally shook herself and scrubbed the goosebumps that ran down her arms.

She mustn't let him see her fear.

Tessa scanned the room. "I will need two tables about five feet apart over there by the window—one for my supplies and one for Violet to pose on. Once that is done, I will set up my easel. Then we can slide the trunk next to my work table. The window, though filthy, will provide some light, but I will required three lanterns—one beside Violet and two on my work table."

Jared snapped his fingers again. "You heard her. Do as she says."

The men scrambled around and soon set the stage to Tessa's satisfaction. When she stooped to unlatch the trunk, her stomach rumbled so loudly, she clutched her midriff.

Violet snorted. "Someone is hungry."

"I tend to get so wrapped up in my art that I often miss meals. I imagine Stephen and the boys, especially Adam, are starving. An acquaintance once compared the boys to pharaoh's locusts."

Violet giggled. "I sent them bread and cheese an hour ago."

"You are kind. I should like to be with them, if that is permitted. We'll begin the painting this evening." Tessa studied Violet and cocked her head. "Please, leave your hair down and wear a dress."

"I have a purple one. Will that do?"

"I'm sure it will be perfect, but if it doesn't suit, I can always make it whatever color we choose. That's the beauty of paint."

Tessa lifted a clay pot from her supply chest, pried open the cork top, and sniffed the contents.

Jared stepped closer. "What is that?"

Caught off guard, Tessa jerked. Why must he creep up on her?

She pushed the top back onto the pot. "It's walnut oil. I mix it with pigments to create my oil paint. It has a more pleasant smell than turpentine, though it tends to go rancid faster than turpentine or linseed oil." She positioned the pot next to a pile of rags. "It's good for cleaning brushes too."

"Interesting," said Jared, though he stared at her and not the clay pot.

Tessa detested Jared's relentless leers and innuendos. Soldiers on constant alert in battle must experience something similar. Fatigue dropped on her shoulders as a heavy mantle. She needed to put her head down and soon. "May I go now?"

The smirk on Jared's face made Tessa nauseous. "Tom, take her back. She does look a bit peaked, and I am certain she prefers the company of her loving husband to ours."

Tom tried to take her elbow, but she jerked away and hurried in front of him to the cell. When he opened the door, she rushed straight into Stephen's waiting embrace.

"You're shaking." Stephen folded his arms around her. "What happened?"

Tessa pressed her cheek into his chest. "N-Nothing. I need you to hold me for a moment."

He curled his arms around her, and she took comfort from his warmth and sturdy frame. The steady beat of his heart drumming next to her ear calmed her own rapid heartbeat.

Stephen stepped back. "Come. Let's sit on the pallets by Adam."

When they reached the cot, Adam made an effort to sit up, but Stephen motioned for him to lie back. "See how much he has improved?"

She tried to smile, but her lips quavered too much. "Yes, I can see. It makes me very happy. But, please, I am weary, and I need to rest before I go back out there."

"Of course. Here, lay your head on me. The boys and I will be as quiet as church mice."

Tessa curled up on the floor, using Stephen's lap as a pillow. Adam slumped back down on the mattress. Francis settled on the floor beside the cot and leaned his back against the wall. In only a few moments, Tessa fell asleep.

She awoke a while later to find the three of them in the exact same positions. It must have been especially difficult for the boys to remain silent. Their consideration made her love them even more.

She stood and stretched out the kinks in her back. "Stephen, is there enough water in one of the buckets for me to sponge bathe?"

"Yes, there's plenty. I'll put it beside the bench. Gentlemen, if you would turn your backs, Tessa will need privacy." He placed the bucket at Tessa's feet and then joined his brothers.

Tessa removed her clothing except for her chemise, then dipped the soap into the water and scrubbed her body, reveling in the fresh lemon smell and the soothing feeling of the suds running down her arms. She used a coverlet to dry off and then donned her clothes, remembering to slip the dagger into her under-pocket.

Seeing her men staring at the wall as still as statues made her smile. "You may turn around. I do so appreciate your consideration."

She unbound her hair and arranged the pins beside her on the bench. She rummaged through her rucksack and retrieved the brush, but it fell out of her hand and slid across the floor.

Stephen picked it up and sat beside her. "May I?"

Surprised, she turned her back to him. He gently swept through her long tresses and then curled tufts of hair around his hand and stroked the ends with the brush. Waves of pleasure surged through her with each movement he made.

"You are good at this," she said, twisting a tendril through her fingers.

"It's my pleasure."

When he was done, he put the brush down on the bench. "Would you like for me to braid it?"

The low timbre of his voice sent ripples down her arms. "You know how?"

He snorted. "I used to braid Knight's mane and tail for parades we were in."

Adam and Francis, who had been watching their brother's every move, stared at each other wide-eyed.

Their brother revealed a side of him they apparently had never witnessed before. Tessa found their astonishment endearing.

When Stephen finished the braid, she wound it into a chignon and pinned it at the nape of her neck. "Thank you. I feel much refreshed."

She reached for her stockings, but Stephen grabbed them first. "May I?"

Her face flushed. "I...yes."

As he glided the rough cotton legging up her calf, the feel of

139

his hands on her skin awakened new and pleasant sensations. Never before had she imagined what a sensual gesture donning stockings could be. When he finished tying the stocking ribbons, he slid her feet into her shoes and laced them.

Suddenly, urgently, he lunged forward, threw his arms around her waist, and pressed his face into her midriff. He gazed up at her, and the adoration in his warm brown eyes melted her heart.

He rose slightly and curled his body around hers to whisper in her ear. "My dearest, I know this is a terrible time and place, but I must take this moment to tell you that I love you with all my heart. I don't know why I haven't said this before. I guess with all that's happened...but I adore you from the top of your glorious golden tresses to your lovely, dainty pink toes."

His words came rapidly, and Tessa's happiness multiplied with each and every one. She cupped his face in her hands, leaned down, and kissed him. The moment their lips touched, a blazing warmth permeated her body.

He was shaking.

He rose up from his knees, sat on the bench, and pulled her onto his lap. "How I have longed to do this." He kissed her with such abandon, her body melted into his.

His lips were surprisingly soft and warm. His strong arms and his tenderly spoken, whispered endearments created a cocoon of intimacy around them.

She leaned back and pressed a hand against his chest. "You've made me so happy, Stephen, for I have loved you these many days."

"You have?" His eyes sparkled. "But that is marvelous."

"Yes, it is. Kiss me again so I may know for sure."

"With the utmost pleasure, my dear one."

The feel of his arms, his smell, the whiskers on his face, his hammering heart—every part of him heightened her bliss.

She twirled the tie string of his shirt around her finger. "When did you know...that you love me?"

"Thinking back on it, I felt an attraction from our first meeting." He twined his fingers through hers. "I look at your lovely hands and tiny wrists and marvel at the skill in them to create stunning pieces of art. It's amazing how you see into people's hearts and reveal their personalities in your sketches. Then there's the caring way you treat my brothers. I don't believe there was one particular moment when I knew for sure that I love you. It crept up on me."

"You make me sound as if I were an invasive vine!"

"Ha! You did invade my heart, my mind, my body."

He smiled, and she drew a line with her finger across the dimple beside his mouth. They chuckled, and she enjoyed the humming of his ribcage against her body.

"And you, my darling. You say you have loved me for days?" He nibbled on her earlobe, sending chills down her arms.

She slipped a finger inside his shirt collar and caressed his chest hair. He sucked in a breath. The sudden rush of power to elicit such a response delighted her.

"Yes. The moment I saw you, I was overwhelmed with the desire to paint your portrait. You are, as women say, *swoon worthy*."

"You jest." Despite his comment, the glint in his eyes told her that her words flattered and pleased him.

She curled a finger around a tress of his hair. "It wasn't your appearance alone. It was the way you behaved with your brothers. The kindnesses you showed me and my father. The adoration you have for Knight."

"I am humbled that a woman like you could regard me so."

She gently touched the healing skin at his hairline, rose up, and kissed it. "I so wanted to do that when I was bandaging it."

They kissed, murmured words of love, and kissed again

until Tessa remembered Francis and Adam, who sat together on the bed.

"Look," she whispered. "They are facing the wall. Are they not the most thoughtful of brothers?"

Stephen laughed aloud. "Francis, Adam, you may turn around now. I thank you for your gallantry."

Tessa and Stephen stood up from the bench, and when they approached the boys, Adam grinned, but Francis scowled.

Stephen coiled his arm around Tessa's waist and pulled her close. "Why do you frown so, Francis? Is something wrong?"

Francis twisted around on the bed. "Please, Tessa, hurry and finish the portrait so that we may leave this room. There are only so many moments of privacy I can endure."

Stephen guffawed and slapped Francis on his back, and they all laughed.

The cell door slammed open, ending their revelry.

"It's time," Tom announced, his expression as sour as ever.

Tessa donned her fresh mobcap, kissed each of her men, and left the room.

Thank You, Lord, for this blessing.

Fortified by their love, she steadied her shoulders, ready to face the enemy.

CHAPTER 20

*R*ays of the late-afternoon sun filtered through the grimy tavern window when Tessa entered the room full of men who had maneuvered their chairs into rows behind her easel as if in a theater.

She was to be the entertainment for the evening.

Someone had attached the garden scene canvas onto the easel and had placed lighted lanterns as Tessa had ordered. Violet sat on a table and had swung her legs over the edge, fetching in her purple satin dress with lacy sleeves and low-cut neckline.

"Violet, if you would, please turn your body sideways and face me. Bend your right knee and put your foot flat on the table. Let your left leg dangle over the edge." Tessa coached her subject with extra gestures as she followed the directions. "Now drape your arms around your knee, as if you are hugging it."

Violet made a pose. "Like this?"

"Perfect." Tessa tilted Violet's head slightly, returned to the canvas, and selected a piece of charcoal. "I'm posing you as if you are sitting on the garden wall."

With a few swift strokes, she created the outline of Violet's body, but after a few minutes, Tessa hesitated. "Will you take your shoes off? I feel you need to be barefooted for this."

"But..." Violet's lavender eyes darkened to purple.

Her obvious reluctance puzzled Tessa. "Come, it will be fine."

Violet complied, but when she exposed her feet, her face grew beet red.

One of the men directly behind Tessa chortled. "Never in my life have I seen such long toes. They're bigger than yours, Walt."

The mocking comments continued, and Tessa regretted her request immediately. They were laughing at Violet, and it was Tessa's fault.

"One moment." She hurried behind the bar, where she gathered cloths and a pan that she filled from a water cask.

She sat on a chair facing Violet and put the pail on a seat next to her. She gently immersed Violet's feet into the water. The astonished men went silent as she lifted Violet's right foot and proceeded to wash it. She massaged her toes and rubbed the bottom of her foot and ankle. She repeated the process with Violet's other foot.

"Why?" Violet, tears pooling in her eyes, barely managed to choke out the word.

"I ask you for your forgiveness for embarrassing you," Tessa whispered. "Christ tells us to humble ourselves. Become another's servant. I'm only following what He taught."

She toweled Violet's feet dry and helped her retain her pose, arranging the hem of her dress to cover all but the tips of her toes. They continued on as if nothing had happened, though Tessa kept glancing over her shoulder, on the lookout for Jared. He entered the tavern a couple of hours later as she put away her pencils and charcoal pieces.

One of the men who preceded him leaned into Violet and whispered, "Careful. He's in a foul mood."

Jared paused at the easel and considered the drawing, bobbing his head and rubbing his forefinger across his chin. "Fascinating. With a few strokes of charcoal, you have pictured my *chérie*'s lovely body perfectly." He turned and stared at Tessa. "I am impressed. Come, have dinner with me."

Violet, who had observed the encounter closely, hopped down from the table and stretched like a contented cat. "Oh, good. This posing is hungry business."

"Not you, Violet. Tonight I dine with our artist. You may go to your bed."

Tessa's stomach muscles clenched, and her heart raced.

The dangerous glint in his eyes precluded any argument, and as Violet left the room, she peered over her shoulder. "Good night, Tessa."

"Good night." Tessa slung her rucksack over her shoulder. "I'm tired myself. I think I should retire as well."

"That is not what I want." He spoke each word deliberately, sliding the rucksack down her arm and onto the floor. "It's time for us to get acquainted."

A lump of panic formed in Tessa's throat. She ran her hand along the front of her petticoats, searching for the knife hidden there.

Would she have to use it? Could she?

Jared motioned to a chair. "Please, be seated. We must wait for our meal to be prepared. One of my men, Beardsley, has a particular talent for cooking."

The men gathered in groups around the tables facing the bar and proceeded to drink, serving themselves since Jared had banished Violet from the room. Some of them played cards, and others tried to hide their curiosity, occasionally glancing at her and Jared.

Jared cocked his head and leaned his elbows on the table, tapping his fingertips together. "How would you like to paint a portrait of me?"

Tessa already knew more about him than she cared to and detested the thought of spending hours alone with him. "I'm afraid my concentration is such that I cannot think of more than one project at a time."

"When you have completed Violet's portrait, then?" His broad smile bared his even white teeth.

She brushed an imaginary piece of lint from her dress. "But my family and I will be gone by then."

He leaned closer. "Perhaps I might...persuade...you to stay."

Tessa understood his meaning. His ogling sickened her.

He toyed with her. She must not let him see how much he frightened her.

Lord, please, give me strength.

A man entered the room and motioned to Jared, who stood and held out his arm to Tessa. "Ah, Beardsley summons us. Our dinner awaits."

She reached for her rucksack, but he waggled his finger at her. "Leave it."

He folded her arm around his, and they followed Beardsley across the tavern, through the store, and into a large apartment. A dining table in the center of the room held two gold candelabras ablaze with multiple candles each. Other lighted candles had been placed on tables and across the fireplace mantel. A bed with intricately carved posts and a massive headboard fit for a king dominated the room. Lush tapestry covers and silk-encased pillows topped the mattress. Tessa tried to avoid staring at the bed, but before she could look away, she spotted the carving of a naked woman on the headboard. Her stomach tumbled.

Jared pulled out a chair and invited her to sit. He had observed her eyeing the bed and had deliberately seated her so that she was forced to face it. He grinned, enjoying her discomfort.

Beardsley approached the table, opened a bottle of wine, and poured a small amount into Jared's glass.

Jared swirled it around, smelled it, and took a sip. "Excellent. I think you will enjoy this, Tessa. It came from the wine cellar of a connoisseur we...ah...visited in Charles Town."

Beardsley *harrumphed*, filled their glasses, put the bottle on the side table, and left the room.

Seeking Dutch courage, Tessa took a sip of the dark-red liquid, and it burned all the way down to her empty stomach.

"I understand you wish to know your subjects before you paint them."

She refused to engage with him.

He sipped his wine and savored it. "My mother was the mistress of a French nobleman. So, for want of a better word, she was a prostitute. I never knew my father. One evening...I was eleven, as I recall...her benefactor was beating her, and I tried to step in. It angered him so much that he had me kidnapped and put aboard a pirate ship bound for the Barbary Coast. I served on that ship for nearly ten years, selling slaves and raiding settlements from Africa to the English Channel. I escaped and, because I had my fill of sailing, I came here to the colonies. *Et voilà!* I am as you regard me today."

"What a tragic life you have led."

Someone else may have engendered Tessa's sympathy, but not him. He had caused too many others to suffer, including herself.

"On the contrary, my life has been one of adventure. And at a profit, I might add." He rose and pulled her chair out from the table. "Come, see." He led the way to a long, low cabinet laden with chests of every size and shape.

He swept his hand over the treasures. "Pick one."

She pointed to a small cedar chest. He opened it and withdrew a necklace fashioned of gold and with emeralds the size of marbles. He stood behind her, lifted the necklace over her head, let it rest on her skin, and attached the clasp.

Tessa shivered from the cold weight and from the touch of his hands as he turned her around.

He frowned. "I don't like it. They are much too garish for you. I must find something more suitable. Pearls, perhaps?" He snapped his fingers. "Or, much better, blue diamonds to match your eyes."

"I don't want anything from you." Had she truly said those words aloud?

He slunk around in front of her and tipped up her chin, forcing her to meet his gaze. "But I want something from you, my dear."

He moved closer, wafting the aroma of tobacco and wine about her. His arms snaked around her waist. She shuddered and pressed her hands against his chest.

"Come, Tessa. Don't resist. Make yourself softer for me," he cajoled.

She slipped her hand through the slit in the side of her skirt and into the under-pocket.

Jared grabbed her hand just as her fingers touched the dagger. He slid a hand across her stomach, across the outline of the knife sheath. "What is this? Some sort of weapon? You surprise me, chérie. You have more spunk than I thought. Good. It will heighten our pleasure."

Just as Tessa wished she could melt down into the floor and disappear, two men slammed open the door and stormed into the room. Tom followed them, and the fear in his wide eyes was palpable.

"Tom, I gave orders not to be disturbed," Jared shouted, keeping a firm grip around Tessa's waist. His face had gone bloody red.

"Anders wants to see you," one of them said gruffly.

Jared's body trembled with anger. "I haven't dined yet. Tell him I'll come when I'm ready."

Tessa tried to pull away, but his vice-like grip held her fast.

The second man scowled. "He says, come now. There's a boat on its way downriver tomorrow. Full of loot but heavily guarded. It will take all of us, and we need a plan."

Jared freed Tessa, and she quickly stepped away. Close to fainting, she gripped the table with both hands.

"Tom, escort Mrs. Griffith back to the cell. I want everyone with me except Landers and Perry, who'll guard the place." He pulled Tessa close once more, turned her hand over in his, and kissed her palm. "Until tomorrow, then."

Back in the cell, Stephen met her at the door with open arms.

She scrubbed her hand against her skirts and shook so hard she found it difficult to speak. "He-he kissed my hand. I cannot bear that he touched me," she muttered.

Stephen clasped her hand. "Show me where."

When she turned her palm up, Stephen kissed it again and again, wiping away the memory of Jared's kiss and branding her with his own.

She leaned into him and whispered, "He intends to...to...do me harm."

"My darling, I'm here." He wrapped his arms around her and held her tightly.

"Why are you whispering?" asked Francis, who balanced on the edge of the cot next to Adam.

Stephen let go of Tessa and paced up and down, worry lines etched into his face. "We must get out of here. I fear what Jared might do." He stopped pacing. "We must make a plan. There's never more than one guard with Violet. We could attack him."

Francis stood. "We could, Stephen, but how would we escape out of the building? We would have to somehow get past all those men."

Tessa clasped Stephen's sleeve. "We may not have to. I think they are about to leave."

The cell door key rattled, and Violet entered. "I heard you and agree we have to get you out of here." She glanced at Tessa. "And soon. I have a plan. All the men have gone but two. I have sleeping draughts that I will serve them in a few minutes. It won't take long to work." She handed Tessa her rucksack. "I filled this with a canteen full of the cinchona tea, food, bandages, and the other medicines Adam will need."

Tessa draped the rucksack over her shoulder. "It's very heavy."

"There's also a pistol and ammunition."

"Let me carry it." Stephen lifted it off Tessa's shoulder and put it on the bench.

Violet turned and cracked open the door. "I'll return when it's time. Be ready."

"Before you go, we need to pray." Stephen gathered everyone into his embrace.

At first, Violet hesitated, but after a few moments, she squeezed in between Francis and Tessa.

Huddled next to her men and Violet, Tessa listened to her husband thank the Lord for his family and for the many blessings they had received. He beseeched the Lord for grace, mercy, wisdom, and strength. When he finished, they each echoed his *amen.*

"You truly meant what you prayed, Stephen?" Violet asked, lines furrowing her brow.

"I did."

Violet's eyes held deep pools of sadness. "I wish we had more time to talk about Jesus. He seems to have had much hand in making each of you the lovely people you are." She closed the door behind her.

Adam and Francis sat together on the cot. On the bench,

Tessa laced her fingers through Stephen's, leaned against his shoulder, and waited in silence.

Though it seemed longer, less than an hour passed before Violet unlocked the cell and motioned for them to follow. As they crept down the hallway, Violet led the way and carried the rucksack while Stephen and Francis supported Adam, who was still too weak to walk on his own. Tessa, at the rear of the group, held her breath for so long, she could barely put one foot in front of the other.

They reached the bar where both guards had splayed their drugged bodies across a table. One snorted so loud, Tessa tripped over her own feet. She grabbed a chair, righted herself, and then scurried after the others out the front door and into the yard near the tether line.

"I have saddled two horses," said Violet. "They were the only ones in any shape for travel—your horse, Mr. Griffith, and one other. I'm afraid you'll have to double up."

Stephen threw his arms around Knight's neck before he mounted and pulled Adam up in front of him. Tessa climbed on the other horse behind Francis and wrapped her arms around his torso. He shook and his breath came in uneven gasps.

Tessa patted his back. "Courage, Francis," she whispered.

"Thanks, Tessa. I'm about to jump out of my skin."

Violet handed the rucksack to Stephen. "You still have several hours before dark. I suggest you ride back to Fort Hampton, but do not take the road. The outlaws are gathering and will be using it."

Tessa gripped the sides of Francis's shirt. "Are you sure you won't come with us, Violet? What will happen to you? Will you be punished for helping us?"

"My life is here. Jared and I have been together going on ten years. I know how to handle him. Now, go. You don't have much time."

They galloped across the clearing and entered the gloomy forest, so thick the tree branches blocked most of the sunlight. Tessa turned and waved to Violet, who hovered in the doorway.

Lord, keep her safe, please. And may she find her way to You.

"Stephen, how do we know we're going in the right direction?" Francis asked, lowering his voice.

"If we keep parallel to the road, we'll be traveling north. When it gets dark, if there's a clearing once in a while and some bright stars, I know how to navigate using them. We can also use the streams for guidance, as they flow south. We travel upstream. Try to remember that, Francis, if we should ever get separated."

Tessa panicked. "But that won't happen. We will stay together, won't we?"

"Don't fear, dearest. I mention these things as a precaution, and my brothers must learn how to manage in this wilderness."

His steady voice calmed her immediately but not as much as the sweet pleasure of his calling her *dearest*.

They wound their way through patches of trees, over rocky terrain, and across grassy meadows flush with wildflowers. They skirted thorn bushes that reached out and tore Tessa's stockings, leaving streaks of blood down her legs. Though they rested the horses often, the exhausted animals grew sluggish, and foam covered their bodies.

They stopped beside a stream long enough to share the bread and cheese Violet had packed for them and wash it down with the cool water. Tessa splashed her face and arms but flinched when the water burned the scratches on her arms.

They continued on as fast as they dared. Adam grew visibly weaker with each passing mile. What should she be doing to help him? Try as she might, she could not stop looking over her shoulder.

After riding a few more miles, they dismounted in a clearing, and Stephen laid Adam against a fallen tree. "His fever has returned."

Tessa felt Adam's forehead and cheeks with the back of her hand. "I fear so. Some tea might help." She held the canteen to Adam's lips, and he managed to gulp down several mouthfuls.

"We're awfully close to the road, Stephen. I can see it there." Francis pointed past a break in the trees.

"I—" Stephen put his finger to his lips.

The sound of horses' hooves approached from two directions. Tessa shivered. When the riders stopped only a few yards away, the hair on her arms tingled. She, Francis, and Stephen crouched down beside Adam. Knight raised and lowered his foot. Sweat beads rolled down Tessa's back. She could not make out the number of men. Could they hear her heart pounding? Their voices traveled clearly.

"Jared is crazed. Ordered us not to come back without his prisoners," said one man.

"What's so special about them?"

"They know about the wagon train attack."

One man snorted. "I heard he'd taken a fancy to the woman."

"Must be close to thirty of us searching. I hope we catch 'em soon. Don't want to miss out on the boat."

Tessa's leg muscle cramped with pain so sharp, she nearly screamed. Why wouldn't they hurry up and leave?

"They're bringing out the hounds. That's sure to flush them out."

"Well, we ain't going to find them hanging around out here."

Tessa waited for them to ride back down the trail before she breathed in deeply and stretched out her leg. She massaged the aching muscle. She stood up gingerly and paced back and forth, releasing the cramp. The knot in her stomach would not release as easily.

"It will be dark soon. We need to move on," Stephen said, his voice hoarse from tension.

They had traveled another hour when the baying of hounds sounded in the distance.

"They will pick up our trail soon." Stephen led them down an embankment into a dry creek bed. He stopped in front of a small cave the water had sliced out from under the roots of a pine tree. "Let's lay Adam in there."

Once they took the supplies from Tessa's rucksack, placed them in the cave, and made sure Adam was comfortable, the three of them met outside.

Stephen folded his arms across his chest. "He's too ill to go on, and the horses are spent. It's only a matter of time before the hounds reach us."

Tessa hugged her arms across her body.

Francis hunched his shoulders. "We can't give up. Can we?"

"There's one tactic." Stephen looked away.

Guessing the tactic, Tessa shook from head to toe.

Stephen reached out and squeezed her hand. "We can separate."

"No. No. That can't be our only choice." Tessa pressed her hands to her face.

Stephen gently pulled her hands away from her face and held her tightly. He stepped back, tilted her chin, and kissed her.

Would this be their last kiss? Tessa's chest felt hollow.

Stephen placed his hands on her shoulders. "You and Francis must make your way northwest and then cut back northeast to the fort. Adam cannot go on. He and I will remain here. We have one hope. I will charge the horses south, and maybe...just maybe...they will divert the chase away from us."

Tessa began to cry. "I cannot abide this."

"Courage, my darling girl. The plan just might work." He

kissed her forehead. "Let's pray it does, and we'll meet you at the fort."

He approached Knight and, murmuring words of endearment, stroked the horse's neck and shoulders. He positioned Knight side by side with the other horse and then yelled and whooped and slapped them on their haunches, driving them away. Knight followed the panicked horse, and they galloped up the embankment. Yards away, the loyal mount hesitated, turned, and bobbed his head.

"Go-o-o! Get out of here. Now!" Stephen shouted, waving his arms frantically. The bright moon overhead revealed the tears that streamed down his face.

Knight galloped away, and Tessa's heart broke at the sound of his hooves thundering through the woods.

It is my turn to be pushed away.

Stephen faced his brother. "Francis, take care of your sister. Remember what I've taught you about navigating."

"Yes, Stephen." Francis choked on the words and entered the cave with Tessa to bid Adam goodbye.

At the cave entrance, Stephen gathered Tessa into his arms. "My precious, precious one. We don't know what is in store for us. We haven't had much time together, but the love we share will sustain us through anything. We must put on the armor of God, and I promise you with all my heart that no matter what occurs, we will be together, whether it be here or in eternity." He cuddled the back of her head with his hand. "Now kiss me, my darling, one more time."

She rose up on her tiptoes, and her tears mingled with his as they kissed goodbye. Was this how it felt when one's heart broke?

Francis accepted Stephen's bear hug, squared his shoulders, and clasped Tessa's hand. "Let's go."

As they ran, she ached to look back, but if she did, she might never leave. Francis guided with confidence, often assisting her over rocks and fallen logs. Long strands of her hair came loose and caught on limbs. He patiently untangled her hair, taking care not to harm her. Briars gouged the sides of her rucksack and ripped her petticoats. Low-lying branches tore one of her sleeves. Francis fared no better, losing a sleeve and part of his waistcoat.

They reached a shallow creek and hopped from rock to rock, but when she tried to scale the embankment, she suffered a crippling stitch in her side.

"Francis, we must stop. I cannot breathe."

He hauled her up the hill and dropped her onto the ground. "I am the same. I feel I may vomit. We can rest and then go a bit slower. Conserve our energy."

The moon cast a blue-gray glow and formed eerie shadows on the ground. The bright beacon helped them avoid obstacles instead of leaping over or running through them. They lessened their breakneck pace and traveled more deliberately. A wolf howled in the distance, his lonely lament reverberating throughout the woods.

"We must find shelter soon." Sucking in gulps of air, Francis bent over and leaned his hands on his knees.

The snort of a horse shot a wave of dread through Tessa's body.

"Over there. Hide there." Francis grabbed her arm and steered her toward a tunnel formed by a massive laurel bush.

They ducked down and climbed underneath the branches and laid still, barely daring to breathe.

"Come out," a voice called to them.

CHAPTER 21

essa and Francis crawled out of the tunnel to face two Indians sitting astride their ponies.

She peered around Francis, who had stepped in front of her. "I know you. You are scouts from Fort Hampton." Her body sagged with relief.

"And you are the Griffiths who cause much trouble," said one of the men whose gold earrings reflected the moonlight. "I am Tala and this is Doya."

"I am Tessa and this is my brother-in-law, Francis."

The baying of the hounds echoed nearby. Tessa flinched. Had they discovered Stephen and Adam's hideout?

"We must go." Doya stretched out his arm to Tessa and lifted her up behind him.

"Wait," Tala ordered.

Tala dismounted and retraced Francis's and Tessa's footsteps, spreading the contents of a leather pouch on the ground.

"What is he doing?" Francis asked.

Doya grinned. "Spreading black pepper. It will spoil your scent. You made a path a child could follow."

Francis squared his shoulders. "I've never had an occasion to disguise my path."

"I could teach you." Doya pressed a hand to his heart, a gesture that removed the sting from his words.

Francis relaxed. "Thank you. I would like that."

Tala mounted his horse and pulled Francis up behind him, and they rode deeper into the forest.

"Where is Mr. Griffith?" Tala asked over his shoulder.

"My brother stayed behind with our other brother who is too sick to travel."

What was happening to them? The thought of the outlaws capturing them made Tessa heartsick.

Francis turned toward the direction of their flight. "Could we go back and get them?"

Tala guided their horse around a thicket. "No. Too many men fill the woods. More than fleas on a dog. Colonel Stanton means to wipe out the outlaws for all time. For miles around, his soldiers flush them out like rats."

And Violet?

Doya shoved a low-hanging branch up out of their way. "Word is, outlaws hunt your family. Why?"

"We are witnesses to the fact that they attacked our wagon train and tried to make it look like Indians did it," Francis answered.

"Evil men." Doya tapped his feet against his horse's sides.

They traversed a shallow creek, and Tessa tightened her arms around Doya. "Do we ride for the fort?"

"No." Doya patted her hand. "Too dangerous. As I said, too many outlaws. We head for our village."

They traveled for miles in silence until Tessa sensed a decrease in the tension, and their stops for rest grew longer. They dismounted beside a stream, and Tala left them, later returning with three rabbits he had killed.

Were they safe now?

Tala answered her unspoken question when he lit a fire to cook the rabbits. When the rabbits were done, Francis, apparently too hungry to wait for them to cool, grabbed a piece of the meat and devoured it.

Francis wiped his hands on his breeches. "This is the tastiest food I've ever eaten."

Tessa savored a morsel. "I agree."

"Does anyone want that last piece?" Francis asked, eying the rabbit left on the branch spit.

Doya and Tala stopped eating and grinned at each other, transforming their fierce, warrior-like countenances.

"Eat," Tala answered, staring up at the sky. "We sleep here tonight. Our village is a half day's ride away."

Tessa lay on her back, watching the white coals of the fire breathing their last breath of the night.

Thank You, Lord, for this day...for my family and the love we share...and for these men who risk their lives to care for us. Please, keep Stephen and Adam safe.

Her eyelids grew heavy, and she had almost fallen asleep when Tala, who lay on the opposite side of the fire, called her name.

"Why do you cling to the bag you carry?" he asked.

She pulled her rucksack closer. "It contains many treasures. Many precious memories."

"I can see? Or is it a secret?"

She sat up and handed him the bag.

He laid it across his lap, pulled out sketches, and held them up to the dim firelight. "You made these?"

She nodded.

"The Great One has blessed you with a mighty gift. I'm honored that you would share with me." He returned the sketches and handed the bag back to her. "A great treasure."

He touched the small leather pouch that hung from a piece of rawhide underneath the silver gorget that covered his heart.

"I, too, carry treasures here in my medicine pouch. Tokens that have sacred meanings known only to me. It is good that we share this. Yes?"

"Yes, Tala. It is good." She lay back down and fell into a fitful sleep. Her last conscious thought was of Stephen and the desolation on his face as he bade her goodbye.

CHAPTER 22

*I*nside the cave underneath the pine tree, Stephen held the canteen for Adam to take the last swallow of tea. He unwrapped the bandage around his brother's arm and released a soft, thankful breath. Even in the dim light of the cave, he could tell that most of the angry skin was no longer puffy with infection. He spread honey over the wound and covered it with fresh bandages.

Adam lay back on the ground with a groan, his body shaking from head to toe. "I am sorry to be so much trouble."

"You concentrate on getting well. Try to think about training horses. I know you love them as much as I."

Stephen tucked the pistol into his waistband and stepped outside where the full moon shown bright as a beacon, lighting the dry creek bed and casting shadows among the trees. Pacing back and forth across the sand, he attempted to devise a plan. Men's voices close by stopped him in his tracks. He bolted into the cave and readied the pistol.

"We can see you in there," said one man.

"Griffith? That's you, ain't it?" came another familiar voice.

Stephen peered between the dangling tree roots and recognized Jefferson and Reynolds walking toward him, leading their horses and mules.

He blew out a big breath and turned back to Adam. "It's our friends. The trappers." He climbed out and clapped their backs. "Am I happy to see you."

Reynolds bent over and stared into the cave. "What's the matter with Adam? Where's Tessa and Francis?"

"It's a long story—" At the *crack* of a musket, Stephen ducked in time to dodge a bullet that streaked by him and buried into the embankment.

"What the—" Jefferson yelled and crouched down behind his horse.

"Coming from yonder...to our left," said Reynolds, pointing into the trees.

"I see 'em." Jefferson slid two muskets off the mule, aimed and fired one, and threw the other to Reynolds.

Jefferson grabbed a bag of cartridges, rammed one into the barrel, and fired.

Stephen gaped. "That's faster than I've ever seen anyone load and fire."

"How many do you see?" Reynolds yelled.

"Five...maybe seven. Too many, for sure." Jefferson fired his musket. "One less now."

Stephen crawled farther out of the cave still holding his pistol at the ready. "I'll go this way, to our right. Make sure they don't surround us."

Another shot and Jefferson's hat flew off his head and sailed through the air. He picked it up from the ground and put his finger through the hole. "Now I'm mad. That was my new hat."

Stephen, his body tingling with renewed energy, spotted the silhouette of a man skirting from tree to tree, but not in range of his pistol. "Pass me the musket," he said to Jefferson, who hunkered behind him.

He grabbed the musket and leveled it. "Aim small, miss small," he muttered the training mantra. He pulled the trigger, and his target fell to the ground.

At that moment, all went silent.

"I don't like this," whispered Jefferson, who crouched low to the ground.

Reynolds shoved the ramrod down the musket bore. "Me neither. They're up to something. I can hear 'em rambling around. Are they fixin' to storm us?"

Stephen moved to turn his back to the front of the cave and braced himself. "Courage, Adam. Know that I love you."

Adam rolled onto his side. "I love you, Stephen."

A picture of Tessa came to mind. She sat beside a campfire sketching, her face a study of concentration.

What a lovely gift from God to have had in his life for even a brief time.

Someone yelled, followed by running noises and then something strange.

Stephen cocked his head. "It's a bugle."

A volley of muskets rang out after the bugle call.

"Ha! You betcha it is. Watch those rats scatter." Jefferson threw his tattered hat into the air.

In minutes, a group of soldiers surrounded them, pointing their bayonets.

"Stand down," ordered their sergeant. "I know these men."

"Phew! Never been happier to see anyone in my born days," Reynolds said, shaking the sergeant's hand.

"You're welcome. We need to get you back to our temporary command post. You stay out here and you might get shot by mistake. It's mayhem."

"I'll need a horse to transport my brother." Stephen indicated the cave opening behind him.

The sergeant motioned to one of the soldiers. "There's plenty of them running around in the woods."

Stephen, Jefferson, and Reynolds fashioned a travois and attached it to the horse one of the soldiers brought. Stephen carried Adam out of the cave and settled him on the travois that was covered in a layer of soft green pine needles. Before mounting the horse, he paused at the edge of the cave, closed his eyes, and envisioned the last time he saw Tessa. She and Francis were holding hands and running through the forest. Once again, he experienced the desolation of letting her go and not knowing if he would ever hold her in his arms again.

I'll find you, my darling. I'll get Adam to safety and come after you, I promise.

~

*J*ust as the sunrise burned away the early-morning mist that lingered over the forest floor, Stephen halted the travois in front of the tavern that had been the outlaws' hideout. Thank the Lord, a British flag now marked it as a temporary command post.

"What's that ruckus?" Jefferson scanned the yard.

Reynolds pointed to a tether line. "The horse over there is going crazy."

Adam sat up on the travois and hung his legs over the edge. "Stephen! It's Knight."

"Ha!" Stephen vaulted from his horse and raced across the yard. When he reached Knight, he squeezed the excited horse around his neck. "Dear boy, I thought I might never see you again." He ran his hands over Knight's body. "Nothing hurt. You are all right. God is good."

With his injured arm clasped to his chest, Adam slowly made his way to Knight and caressed the horse's nose that nuzzled him in welcome. "I am so happy for you, brother. Now, if we can find Tessa and Francis, our family will be whole again."

Knight pawed the ground with his right foot. Stephen ran his fingers down the leg and lifted it to examine the hoof. All was well. "My plan is to get you settled here with the army. And I am hoping they will escort you back to Fort Hampton. Reynolds and Jefferson have agreed to help me search for Tessa and Francis, so the fort will be a good meeting spot for us."

Adam's shoulders drooped. "I wish I could go with you."

Stephen put his hand on his brother's back. "I know, but you must get well. Once we're all together again, we still have several weeks' travel to Camden and a new life to start there."

He meant his words to encourage Adam but welcomed the tiny lift of his own spirits.

They entered the tavern, and Stephen's steps faltered. Tessa's canvases and art chest were stacked in a corner. At least they had not thrown them away.

Once Stephen saw Adam settled in a chair, he joined Colonel Stanton, who was seated at a table at the far end of the room.

"Colonel." He greeted him with a salute.

The colonel nodded. "What brings you here, Griffith? I thought you'd be close to Camden by now."

"It's a very long story, but we ran into outlaws not long after we left the fort. They held me and my family prisoner here."

He frowned, tilting his bewigged head. "Why would they imprison you?"

"We know they are the ones who attacked our wagon train and made it to look as if the Indians did it."

The colonel harrumphed. "Hard to imagine people so depraved."

"We escaped but were separated. My wife and brother are still missing." Stephen rested his arm on the pistol at his waist. "I'd like to ask a favor."

The colonel leaned back in his chair. "Yes?"

"The trappers, Jefferson and Reynolds—"

165

"I'm familiar with them. Good men."

"They want to help me search for my wife and brother. So I ask that my brother, Adam, who is recovering from an illness, be allowed to remain here with you and later be escorted to the fort."

The colonel stood, a deep wrinkle furrowing his brow. "We are returning to the fort tomorrow, and I'm sorry to say, I cannot allow your search."

Stephen started to protest, but the colonel held up his hand.

"We still have troops running down the last of the outlaws. You could get in their way. Be killed by accident. Besides, I have the leader of the rogues, Jared, imprisoned at the fort. We plan to try him, and I need your testimony."

Stephen's frustration nearly overwhelmed him. Every day, every minute he delayed his search meant a bigger threat to Tessa and Francis. He balled up his fists. "I will give you three days. Then I'm going to search for my family, no matter what." How long could Tessa and Francis survive in the forest, surrounded by danger and privation? His gut twisted.

The colonel dropped his chin onto his chest. "I understand. I would insist on the same myself."

"Colonel." Stephen pointed to the canvases. "Those belong to my wife. I'd like to load them into our wagon that I see is still here. I'll need horses to pull it to the fort."

"You have my approval." He walked over to the canvas and studied the drawing of Violet. "Your wife is gifted. It's a shame about the woman, though. She was a diamond of the first water, and this would have been a stunning portrait."

Stephen frowned. "What are you saying?"

"When my troops attacked the tavern, the outlaws put up quite a fight—I'll grant them that. But many died, including this woman. They are buried in a mass grave near the edge of the forest."

"That is sad news, indeed. If it hadn't been for her, we could not have escaped."

The hollow in Stephen's chest ached.

My Tessa will be sad when she hears this.

CHAPTER 23

*T*ala, Doya, Francis, and Tessa entered a patch of rivercane on a trail Tessa could barely discern. The thick cane branches formed a tunnel that blocked the afternoon sun and turned the air cool against her skin. A stream gurgled nearby, but the dense growth concealed it. The black moist soil cushioned the horses' hooves and smelled like a sulfur stick when lit.

Francis, who rode ahead of her, twisted around. "Tessa, this place has a strange feeling about it. Not fearful, but ancient."

"It is stirring. It makes me want to paint."

They followed the path until it opened out onto a clearing with rows of cabins lined on either side. The dwellings were fashioned out of rivercane covered in plaster made of clay, grass, and deer hide. Smoke curled up through holes cut in cedar shingles and lingered in the air between the cabins.

Women sitting on the ground outside their cabins ceased their weaving and waved, expressions of curiosity on their faces. Children ran toward Doya and Tala but stopped when shyness overtook them. The scouts helped Tessa and Francis dismount in the middle of the row of cabins.

"Here comes *ghi gua*, Beloved Woman." Doya indicated a striking woman walking up the path followed by two young women.

Tessa had witnessed noblewomen in England who did not move with as much authority and grace. Long streamers of fringe decorated the hem and shoulders of her bronze-colored dress made of hides beaten to resemble cotton. Diamond-shaped patterns in red and blue embellished the bodice. She wore a wide choker made of rows of white and blue beads, which fit tightly to her neck. A single swan feather adorned her long braids. But her lovely dark-brown eyes captured Tessa's attention. Their lively depths held much wisdom and character.

The woman addressed Doya in their language, but Tessa caught her own name amidst the conversation.

Doya changed to English. "Ghi gua, this is Tessa Griffith and her brother, Francis. They ask for refuge among us."

Tessa curtsied and Francis bowed.

Ghi gua tilted up Tessa's chin and observed her face. "Lovely. You have caring, honest, clear eyes. A pretty blue."

She moved close to Francis and studied him. "There is strength in you."

He bowed his head, seeming moved by her compliment.

"You are both welcome." She pointed to her companions. "This is Ama, which means *water* in our language. And this is Dustu...*spring frog*."

Both young women smiled. When Francis presented them with a formal bow, Dustu giggled. Francis caught her glance and appeared almost thunderstruck. Tessa looked back and forth between them as a sweet tension permeated the air.

"Ama and Dustu, please take Tessa to the water and find fresh clothing. Find ointment for her scratches. Doya, do the same for Francis."

For the first time in hours, Tessa regarded her own and

Francis's appearances. "We are a terrible sight to behold. Our clothes are tattered beyond repair. I am filthy." She touched the side of her hair. Most of it had loosened from the braids and hung in oily strings down to her waist. "I'm sorry we have come to you in such a state."

The woman touched Tessa's cheek. "You have suffered much. And not only physically. We will try to restore you."

Ama and Dustu escorted Tessa through the village past young girls winnowing wheat and watching after the much younger children as they collected tinder. Older men wielded hatchets in carving strips of wood from a huge log. Young men gathered in groups crafting a strange weapon made from a length of rivercane and fashioning darts from thistle.

"What is that?" Tessa asked, pointing to the cane.

"A blowgun," Dustu explained. "For hunting small animals...rabbits and squirrels."

One of the men lifted a cane pole and blew on the end, shooting out a dart that plunged into a straw target. The others cheered and slapped him on his back.

"Astonishing," said Tessa.

This new and exciting world presented marvelous sights and sounds with every turn.

Tessa, Dustu, and Ama soon reached one of the cabins, where Ama retrieved a pile of clothing and blankets and then continued on far from the cabins where the path emptied out onto a river.

"Rain not come for days. The water isn't swift, but is cold," Ama said, lifting her dress over her head and exposing her naked body.

Face heating, Tessa stared at her toes. When Dustu removed her clothes, Tessa swallowed hard.

"Come," said Dustu, "we must rid you of those."

Ama whispered to Dustu and they giggled.

"Ama says your face bears the look of a terrified rabbit. Don't trouble. No one will come close. You are safe."

Did they realize what they required of her? She had rarely ever been naked anyplace in her life...even her bath. She dropped the rucksack from her shoulder and slowly removed her shoes and stockings. She untied her bodice and removed it and her petticoats and stood in her shift. With much encouragement, she removed that, and covering herself the best she could with her arms and hands, she followed them into the water.

Cold was not how she would have described the frigid water that made her squeal. After a time, her body acclimated to the temperature and to the stinging, burning sensation along her thorn-shredded arms and legs. The women lathered her hair with something that smelled like honeysuckle, massaging it into her sore scalp. Back on shore, they wrapped themselves and Tessa in blankets and sat on a patch of thick green grass.

"What is that?" Dustu pointed to a sketch that had slid out of Tessa's rucksack.

Tessa showed her the drawing she had done of the newlywed couple on the wagon train. The memories of that horrible day came rushing back. It made her sick to think of the people whose lives had been cut short. She missed her father terribly.

Dustu's mouth flew open. "You did this?"

Tessa nodded. "And others. Would you like to see?"

The women took their time studying each drawing, more and more awed.

"You would draw my mother?" Dustu asked.

Tessa pushed the pile of sketches back into the bag. "I'd love to, but I'm afraid I don't have any more paper."

The women spoke excitedly to each other in Cherokee. Their bright eyes flashed.

As Tessa sat on the blanket, the sun soaked deep into her

bones. Her eyelids grew heavy, but when Dustu combed and plaited her hair into two long braids that draped over her breasts and down to her waist, she rallied. After donning their clothes, the women wrapped a deerskin skirt around Tessa's waist and tied it with a rope. They pulled a flower-patterned linen shirt over her head. The bell-shaped sleeves came to her elbows, and the hem reached mid-thigh. They slid moccasins onto her feet and tied a beaded belt around her waist.

Tessa fingered the belt and admired its intricate pattern of mountains and birds. "It's lovely."

"Dustu does good hand weaving," Ama said, pointing to the water pattern of her own belt.

Dustu cinched the belt. "I would teach you, Tessa?"

"Yes. I would love that." Would she be in the village long enough, or would Stephen find her quickly?

The girls motioned for her to spin around and then talked in Cherokee a few minutes. Dustu removed her own shell necklace and clasped it around Tessa's neck. Her generosity brought tears to Tessa's eyes, and they hugged one another as friends.

They left the river and encountered Doya and Francis at the top of the hill. Francis wore a trade shirt over a loincloth, thigh-length fringed leggings, and moccasins. His beaded belt was decorated with strips of rawhide that reached his knees. A wide silver band encircled his forearm. Someone had pulled part of his hair into a queue at his crown and decorated it with hawk feathers.

"You are splendid, Francis," Tessa exclaimed.

He glanced sideways at Dustu and laughed. "I agree. And you look as beautiful as I have ever seen you."

"Come to my cabin," said Doya. "My wife will feed us."

Tessa hugged her new friends once more and waved goodbye, curious to see the inside of Doya's cabin. His wife, Agasga, waited outside to welcome them and to drape aside the deerskin door. Inside comprised two rooms, one with a rope-sprung bed topped with pine needles and a blue blanket with red satin ribbons. A cooking fire dominated the other room that had a hole in the roof to draw out the smoke.

"I say," Francis declared, "it smells grand in here." He moved closer to Agasga, who used a flat wooden spoon to serve the food.

"This is bean bread," she said and handed him a small wooden plank with two packets of food rolled up in corn leaves.

She served Tessa, and then everyone sat on blankets and deerskins that covered the dirt floor.

Doya pulled one of the packets directly from the steam pot and tossed it back and forth until it cooled. "Like this." He unwrapped the leaves, exposing a gray-colored loaf. He broke off pieces of the spongy bread and ate them.

Tessa and Francis followed his instructions.

"Delicious," Francis said with his mouth full and then licked his fingers.

"Manners, Francis," Tessa reminded him. "It is delightful, Agasga. What is in it?"

"Ground corn, brown beans, fat, and a bit of water. I roll the dough into corn leaves and steam them."

"And what is that boiling in the pot?" Tessa asked, breathing in the sweet aroma.

"Kanuchi." Agasga stirred the mixture and smiled at Doya. "My husband likes sweets. It is his favorite. Made from powdered hickory nuts and boiled rice. I will roll the paste into balls later."

"May I have another?" Francis asked, wiping his hand on his shirttail.

Agasga grinned and passed him another bean loaf. "I made many. I remember my young brother at your age. He ate enough to fill the giant holes near the hot springs on the other side of this mountain."

Doya snorted and unwrapped another bean bread that he downed in two bites.

When they finished eating, Doya and his wife tucked rolled-up reed mats under their arms and handed Tessa and Francis each one.

"We sleep outside this night." Doya picked up a straw basket and led the way on the path Tessa had taken earlier, where they were joined by the entire village of about eighty men, women, and children, all carrying mats and blankets. Many toted empty baskets over their arms.

Francis leaned toward Tessa. "Where are we going?"

Tessa shrugged. "I know the river is this way. Isn't this exciting? My heart is pounding."

When the crowd reached the water, they turned upstream just as the sun cast its last rays across a darkening sky.

Walking on the banks of the murmuring river with the wind gently swaying the branches overhead, Tessa heard the call of a mourning dove and a wolf's howl far in the distance. The people shared conversations, but in hushed voices.

I have never felt more alive. Oh, Stephen, you would love this. Where are you, my darling?

They came to a meadow replete with wildflowers. Women spread the blankets and mats and sat with their children, while the men built a fire in the middle of the clearing.

Tessa almost burst with curiosity as she and Francis sat with Doya and Agasga. Sitting cross-legged on his mat, Doya lit his pipe and took a draught. He gathered the smoke and wafted it over the top of his head.

"What is happening?" Tessa asked.

"We await the strawberry moon," Agasga answered, pointing to the moon peeking up over a line of distant cedar trees.

Doya took another draught on his pipe and offered it to

Francis, who shook his head. "If the moon turns pink, it means the strawberries are ripe."

Tessa wrapped her arms around her bent knees and stared into the night sky, where stars popped out like diamonds on a black velvet curtain. So many centuries ago, King David had gazed into the night sky and pondered the place of man in God's plan.

Oh, Lord, how magnificent is Your creation.

They remained in companionable silence until someone shouted.

"What?" Tessa sat up and scanned the crowd.

Agasga grinned. "The moon turns pink."

People hugged each other and clapped and laughed. Several young men and women danced joyfully around the fire. After a short while, everyone settled down.

Tessa lay back down, and, using her folded arms as a pillow, she observed the pink moon, now straight overhead, and whispered a nighttime prayer.

Where are you, my love? My heart is only half of itself without you.

CHAPTER 24

*I*n the early morning a couple of days after arriving at Fort Hampton, Stephen sat in one of the rows of chairs staged to resemble a courtroom in Colonel Stanton's office. Two others joined him in the "gallery"—one man in the front row who leaned his arm across the chair beside him and another one who fidgeted and twisted on a seat in the same row as Stephen.

Adam, still spent from their trek, remained in the guestroom of the Stantons' quarters, where Mrs. Stanton hovered over him as a mother hen.

Stephen's emotions roiled as he awaited Jared's trial. He stared at Jared, seated to the right of the colonel with two guards stationed behind him. Despite the torn and stained state of his flamboyant blue velvet waistcoat and the heavy shackles that chained his arms and legs, he maintained his usual air of smugness and superiority. The monster had imprisoned his family, had terrorized Tessa with his sexual advances, and had ordered the slaughter of innocents. Stephen wanted justice. No, more than that, he wanted revenge.

The day before, ten of the outlaws had stood trial, had been found guilty and sentenced to a firing squad. They had met their deaths at dawn. At last, the time had come for their leader to account for his crimes.

The colonel presided at his desk. To his left, a solitary chair provided a place for witnesses.

The last time Stephen was in this office, he and Tessa had married in a stark civil ceremony made much warmer for Mrs. Stanton's efforts. Tessa had been stunning in her pink satin dress with rosebuds in her gossamer golden hair. He pictured her at other times laughing, crying, joking with his brothers, taking the daring swing out over the river, concentrating on one of her sketches.

My heart, I will find you, and when I do, we will be married in a church with God's blessing. I promise.

The colonel tapped his pistol handle on his desk. "The charges have been read, enumerating the many heinous crimes the accused has committed. I will now ask Mr. Alfred Ryan to come forward."

The man on the front row stood and walked forward. His scruffy mud-stained boots clomped on the floor. The sun had faded his blue shirt to gray in places. Suspenders held up his well-worn pants. Someone who worked hard for a living.

He slumped into the witness chair, his shoulders drooping, his head down. He twisted the brim of his hat in his hands. He stared at the floor and then lifted his face to glare at Jared with palpable hatred.

"Please, Mr. Ryan, would you recount as precisely and briefly as you can your contact with the accused?" instructed the colonel.

Mr. Ryan straightened his spine. "About two months ago, me and my lads, Cal and Willis..." He paused. Sorrow distorted his face. "We was on my farm shoveling hay into the horse troughs when that man"—he pointed to Jared— "came riding up with his gang of men. Without warning or saying anything, they shot my boys right off. Then me. Thinking I was dead, I reckon, they took my horses and livestock, ransacked my house, and rode away without looking back. Thank God, my wife and daughter was away visiting." The man leaned back and shook uncontrollably.

The colonel nodded toward Jared. "Are you sure this was the man?" he asked gruffly.

"As God is my witness. He had on the same blue coat he has on now." Mr. Ryan's voice broke.

Jared made a show of bowing his head to the man.

He mocked the grieving man. Stephen's temper flared. Was there no end to his cruelty?

Mr. Ryan stood and shook his fist at Jared. "My dear boys never done you harm. Why? That's what I want to know. Why?"

Jared shrugged.

Stephen's anger burned as fire. Jared didn't care. He really didn't care.

"May you rot in hell," the grieving man yelled and stomped from the room.

Jared flicked a nonexistent piece of lint from his shoulder.

Colonel Stanton waited for the door to close behind the distraught man. "Mr. Thomas Billings, would you come forward?"

Billings sprung from his chair near Stephen, reached inside his jacket, and pulled out a pistol. "I'll not give testimony. This vermin deserves no trial. He and his men killed my brothers... my brothers." He gulped. "Stole the hides we worked all season for to feed our families."

With his senses buzzing, Stephen slowly rose up and turned toward Billings, who cocked the flintlock and with a trembling hand aimed the weapon at Jared.

Colonel Stanford banged his fists on his desk and roared, "Sergeant!"

One of the guards pushed Jared off his chair at the same

moment Stephen lunged for Billings. Just as the gun fired, Stephen shoved the man's arm upward, and the bullet lodged in the ceiling. Two guards slammed open the door to the room and charged toward Billings, who had dropped the pistol and grabbed hold of Stephen's arm as a drowning man seeking help and started crying.

"Take comfort, Mr. Billings. You will have justice." Stephen patted the man's back until the guards escorted him away and closed the door.

Jared had remained on the floor throughout the emotion-charged scene. The guard yanked him up and shoved him back into the chair.

Stephen's insides shook, but he forced a steely-eyed expression. He would not give Jared the satisfaction of knowing how badly he wanted to hit something, anything, to release the tension that held his body captive.

"I will not tolerate any more outbursts." Once again, the colonel tapped his pistol on the top of the desk. "Next witness, Mr. Stephen Griffith. Approach."

Stephen moved to the witness chair, faced Jared, and locked eyes with him.

The colonel shifted in his chair. "Mr. Griffith, please describe in the clearest, briefest words your contact with the accused."

"I met the accused for the first time in the trading post that was the hideout for his band of outlaws after my wife, my two brothers, and I survived an attack on our wagon train. Only the four of us survived the massacre of eighteen innocent people. My wife's father was among them." The vision of Tessa sobbing over her father's body made Stephen grimace.

"My brother, Francis, was the first to discern that it was not Indians who attacked us, but the outlaws. Francis recognized that the brigands possessed items that had belonged to our fellow travelers. He confronted them. In response, Jared had me and my family imprisoned in a room at the post. It was sometime later that my wife recognized the dress Jared's mistress, Violet, wore as one that had belonged to a wagon train passenger."

Stephen never once looked away from Jared and spotted a muscle working in his cheek at the mention of Violet's name.

Maybe his heart was not dead, after all.

"It was Violet who confirmed the outlaws' crimes when she helped me and my family escape."

Jared smirked. What did the monster have to grin about, and why wasn't he ruffled hearing that Violet had helped Stephen and his family? Stephen barely reined in his desire to wipe the smirk from Jared's face.

"I thank you for your testimony, Mr. Griffith, which was given after great sacrifice to yourself. Go with God as you leave to search for your family."

Stephen bowed to the colonel and was making his way out the door when Jared sprang from his chair, rattling the shackles encasing his wrists and ankles. "It's time for this to end. I'm guilty. Do what you will with me, but stop boring me to death."

Stephen hovered in the doorway as one of the guards pushed Jared back down.

Colonel Stanton rose from his desk. "Very well. The killing of a man is murder. The law implies malice when one man, without any reasonable cause or provocation, kills another. Upon the authority of the king's majesty, I have taken inquisitions, recognizances, and examinations regarding multiple charges of murder, assault, and thievery against the accused."

The colonel moved to attention. "Jared Collins, I find you guilty of heinous crimes against your fellow men and against the peace of our said sovereign lord the king, his crown, and his dignity."

Jared turned his head and caught Stephen's eye. He smiled

broadly as if amused by the proceedings and anticipated with delight the words he knew the colonel would speak.

"Sir, I see no remorse in you. No redeeming repentance. It is therefore my gravest duty in the name of His Royal Majesty King George the Second and of the governor of Virginia, Willem Anne van Keppel, second earl of Albemarle, to sentence you to death by firing squad. To be carried out at first light on the morrow. May God have mercy on your soul."

Stephen hurried out the door. Justice was done. It was time to find his Tessa.

CHAPTER 25

*T*essa awoke at dawn the morning after the strawberry moon to the aroma of freshly steamed bean bread. She lay still under the blanket wet with dew listening to the pleasant sounds of mothers murmuring to their sleeping children to waken and prepare for another day. She sat up and stretched and spotted Francis standing across the field near the fire speaking with Doya and a handful of men. Tala, who had been absent during the day, joined them.

Dustu approached the group and beckoned to one of the men to return to their campfire. Francis stared after her and finally rejoined the conversation.

Francis was becoming a man. And quite an appealing man, like his older brother.

Her heart plummeted at the thought of her beloved. Would she ever hold him in her arms again?

She stood and stretched again, rolled up her grass mat, and greeted Agasga, who was cooking over a small fire. "You arose so early, Agasga. You should have let me help you."

Agasga handed Tessa a leaf of bean bread. "You slept well last night. I didn't want to wake you."

After Tessa ate the bread and sipped water from a clay pitcher, Dustu and Ama and two other women came toward her carrying a large basket. They each wore lovely, shy smiles, and their eyes danced.

Dustu laid the basket at Tessa's feet. "We have a gift."

Tessa opened the birch wood cover of the basket to find it filled with layer upon layer of finely tanned skins that were almost white, some the same size as her sketchpad and others even larger.

"We don't have paper. You can use goatskins?" Dustu's cattail-brown eyes filled with anticipation.

Joy and excitement flowed through Tessa's heart and her fingers tingled. "They are perfect. I-I don't have words. I cannot wait to get started."

Dustu spoke to the other women, who clapped their hands.

After everyone had eaten breakfast, the villagers gathered their baskets and headed upstream. Tessa and Francis followed. About a half hour later, they began laughing and pointing to a spot along the riverbank. Caught up in their enthusiasm, Tessa hurried to the front of the group and discovered an almost acre-sized patch of wild strawberries. Some of the children picked the small round red balls and stuffed them in their mouths. The grownups soon mimicked the children.

Tessa plucked one and rolled it around on her tongue, savoring the sweetness. "Mm. Delicious."

Francis gobbled a handful of berries. "Best thing I've ever eaten," he said with the juice running down his chin.

With her heart light for the first time in weeks, Tessa sat on the side of a hill and started sketching—a father holding his toddler on his shoulders, clasping the boy's chubby little legs; a woman balancing a rivercane basket on her hip; an elderly woman sitting on the ground culling stems and leaves from the berries that filled her willow basket. Tessa's hand danced across the goatskins. After a while, a small crowd collected around to watch in awe as she brought their friends to life with her charcoal and pencils.

Doing the activity she loved most in the world made the day race by. When everyone had collected their bounty of berries, they returned to the campsite to spend another night.

As the sun set behind pink and fiery-orange clouds, Dustu sat on a blanket with Tessa and Francis and conversed with him as casually as if they had known each other years.

They were sweet together. But from two different worlds, which was of no consequence to Tessa. What would Stephen say?

The fire turned to coals, and Dustu's mother motioned for her daughter from a nearby campfire.

"Tomorrow?" Dustu waved goodbye.

Francis waved and watched her until she joined her family. "Tessa? May I ask you something...personal?"

"Of course. We are sister and brother now." She sensed what he would ask.

"How does one know if they are in love?"

His handsome brown eyes reflected such sincerity and insecurity, Tessa wanted to hug him.

"I can rely only on my experience with Stephen and, in a less intense way, with that of my parents. It is different for each person, but I do think there are shared reactions."

His brows furrowed. "Reactions? You make it sound as if it is an illness."

She giggled. "Heavens, I don't mean to."

"Go on."

Tessa pursed her lips. "There is the physical attraction part of love where the person's mere presence—their smile, laugh, the sound of their voice, a certain expression—stirs the heart and makes it beat in a way it has never done before."

He pressed a hand to his heart as if checking off an item on that list.

"The attraction builds into passion that is satisfied when two become one—a glorious union between man and wife, as our Lord intended." Tessa lowered her gaze.

She and her beloved had not yet experienced that union. The anticipation that shot through her body almost stole her breath.

"Anything else?" Francis prompted.

"There's the emotional part, too, of course. A feeling of belonging, a connection so intense that when that person is away, their absence creates a painful void...a longing." She smiled at him. "Love is sharing. Their joy makes you happy. Their pain hurts you. You regret their disappointments and rejoice in their triumphs."

"It sounds quite...exciting and yet...frightening."

She reached out and patted his hand. "You've described it perfectly."

"What of the spiritual? What if one person is a Christian and one is not?"

Dear Lord, please, give me wisdom. What should I say?

She chose her words with care. "If one spouse makes Christ the center of their world and one does not, it can cause resentment, frustration, and anger, for as two people are walking the same road, one is looking straight ahead and the other to the right or left. There may be much stumbling and not a lot of peace or rest, especially about how to bring up children."

Francis lowered his head.

Tessa bit her lip. She'd discouraged him. If only Stephen were here. He would do a better job of this for sure.

She drew a quick breath and tried again. "But a nonbeliever can come to know the truth. What a privilege it would be to win an adored one over to Christ through prayer and patience and being a gracious witness."

He scanned the campsite until he spotted Dustu laughing

with her family. "Thank you, dear sister, for your honesty. You've given me much to think about."

He sounded so grown up.

Doya and Agasga, who had been visiting friends, settled down on a blanket they spread by the campfire next to Tessa and Francis.

Doya lit his pipe. "Today Tala scouted the land between here and the fort. There is still much fighting. The outlaws lose, but it's not yet safe to travel. Tala will scout again in two days."

"I wonder where Stephen and Adam are," said Francis. "I'm trying so very hard not to worry, and I pray each day that they are safe."

Tessa patted his hand. "I do the same."

Long after everyone bedded down, Tessa watched the fire until all the embers died.

Was Stephen sitting by a fire or gazing into the same sky? Had Adam recovered?

The night passed peacefully, and the following morning, everyone gathered their belongings and their bounty of strawberries and returned to their homes.

Over the next two days, Tessa joined Dustu in front of Agasga's cabin to learn the intricate craft of hand beading. Francis used one excuse or another to come by often. Though he feigned interest in Tessa's progress, his gaze never wandered far from Dustu.

Tessa spent one afternoon with several elderly ladies who taught her how to weave rivercane baskets. She appreciated their patience as their pretty smiles crinkled their reddish-brown skin and lit their lively almond-shaped eyes. Other women demonstrated how they tanned the goatskins Tessa used for her canvases. When she wasn't learning new skills, she sketched. Keeping her mind occupied made the days go faster and helped her sleep through the nights.

She kept an eye out for Francis who, when he wasn't

learning how to master the blowgun, spent a great deal of time with Dustu, all under the watchful eye of her mother and grandmother.

Agasga commented with a giggle that she caught them making "doe eyes" at each other.

On the fourth night of their visit, Tessa sat with Agasga outside her cabin watching the young women dancing around a bonfire in the center of the village. Dustu especially caught her eye with the graceful swing of her arms and the lithe movements of her body as her moccasin-covered feet tapped out the rhythm. After a time, young men joined the dance, twirling and whirling with vigor that ignited the air. Men circled the fire, keeping time by beating drums of deer rawhide stretched tautly over wooden frames. Some shook rattles of seed-filled gourds, some played rivercane flutes, while others chanted a song. The melancholy sound echoed through the night and sent chills down Tessa's arms. Francis joined in with his harmonica as he watched Dustu dance.

Later, after everyone had dispersed, she, Francis, and Agasga were preparing the bedding on the cabin floor when Doya entered.

"I have news." Doya sat by the fire and lit his pipe. "The outlaws were defeated. So it is safe for you and Francis to return to the fort. Tala and I will go with you tomorrow morning after our meal."

Tessa would soon reunite with her Stephen. Her heart thrummed with joy.

Francis caught Tessa's hand. "Our prayers are being answered."

For a moment, Tessa struggled with conflicting emotions. She wanted with all her heart to be reunited with Stephen... and with Adam...but she had begun to love and admire her new Cherokee friends. Saying goodbye to them would hurt.

Francis's strained expression revealed his own struggle.

Tessa faced their host. "Doya, I cannot thank you and Tala enough for rescuing us. You and Agasga opened your home to us and made us welcome." Tears welled in her eyes. "Once we are settled in Camden, we will make plans to return here as often as possible. If you will have us."

Agasga wiped away her own tears. "Of course, you are family now."

"Stop, women," Doya said gruffly. "Your tears will drown my tobacco."

More tears fell the following morning as the villagers lined either side of the path leading away from the cabins and into the forest, shouting farewells and waving. Some held up the drawings Tessa had made of them. Riding on the horse Doya provided, she waved goodbye.

Thank you, Lord, for blessing me with a new family. Please, may I humbly ask that You help me find my beloved?

CHAPTER 26

The garrison soldiers, having eaten their breakfast, busied themselves with their daily chores. Some cleaned their firearms, or cleared away campfire debris, chopped firewood, built new fires, or relieved the night guards at their stations. Stephen secured the saddlebags on Knight.

Adam stood by his horse nearby, in front of the fort barracks. "Thank you for allowing me to go with you, Stephen. I promise you won't be sorry. I'll keep up."

Adam's plea to come along on the search had won over Stephen's better judgment and delayed their leaving for an additional night. Stephen had avoided Jared's execution the prior dawn, though the volley that delivered the fiend's death had echoed throughout the fort. The world was well rid of that evil.

Stephen checked the horse's cinch and gave Adam a leg up.

Jefferson and Reynolds prodded their horses to either side of him.

"We got your back, Adam." Reynolds tugged on the reins of the mule behind him.

The misgivings about Adam's health, which had been

swayed the day before, came crashing down on Stephen. This could prove to be an arduous journey—nights sleeping on the ground exposed to all kinds of weather, food rationing, long days of riding in the hot sun picking their way through treacherous terrain. He did not care about any of it for himself and would endure every hardship to find his Tessa and his brother for however long it took—days, months, years. But he couldn't risk Adam's welfare in doing so.

Mrs. Stanton, standing in her doorway clasping her husband's forearm, called out, "Godspeed. We're praying you find Tessa and Francis soon...and well."

The colonel's expression was grim. The evening before, the man had warned him of another hazard—the possibility of war. They'd met in the colonel's office studying a map that covered the entire surface of his desk.

"Here"—the colonel had drawn a line across the map with his finger—"is the Upper Ohio River Valley. We claim that it's part of Virginia, but the French claim it as part of New France. Not only is the land of considerable value, but we want the fur trading rights as well."

"So you and your men will be pulled into a war?" Stephen had asked.

"Most assuredly." The man had straightened as he spoke decisively. "I have already begun arrangements to expand the garrison. Once the war begins, and I believe it will be soon—"

Stephen's heart had skipped a beat. "How soon is soon?"

"We're speaking of months. When it starts, settlers from that territory will flee this way. Many in the surrounding areas will want to fort up with us. Then there's the Indian question. I expect the Iroquois Confederacy to side with us. I'm also certain the Cherokee, who control thousands of square miles in the Southern Appalachians, will align with us. The Algonquin — Wabanaki, Ottawaa, Shawnee, Huron—I believe will support the French. You must find Tessa and Francis soon, my friend, and get shored up in Camden. I don't think the hostilities will spread that far, but as for this region, all will be chaos."

Considering what Colonel Stanton had revealed last night, Stephen felt an overwhelming urgency as he mounted Knight and prodded him forward.

What is happening to you now, dear one? Are you safe, hungry, afraid?

He refused to let his mind wander down that path but instead led Adam, Jefferson, and Reynolds out of the fort's gates. They turned southward toward the outlaws' hideout near the last place they had seen Tessa and Francis.

On the two-day ride to the trading post, they stopped by settlements and farms asking people if they had seen or heard about anyone fitting Tessa's and Francis' descriptions, but to no avail.

Considering Adam's health, they spent an entire day and night in a kind farmer's barn avoiding a downpour.

"Will this rain ever stop?" Adam leaned against the barn doorpost. "Each minute that passes means another minute without Francis and Tessa."

Stephen stood beside Adam, his mood as bleak as the sheets of rain blowing sideways across the muddy yard. "We can't give in to exasperation, Adam. Not this early in our search. Remember, we are in this for the duration. For however long it takes."

Adam shrugged. "I know. I'm sorry. I promise not to whine. But where in this world can they be?"

Jefferson, who sat on a hay bale beside Reynolds, called out, "It's a mighty big job we've taken on in a mighty big territory, son. If I've learned anything in my born days, it's that patience and perseverance will win in the end."

Stephen faced the two men, now his revered friends.

"But remember Jesus's teaching about the mustard seed?" Reynolds asked. "If we believe in a merciful, good God and act on that faith, the things we thought were impossible become possible."

"Yep. I've lived through some tough spots that could only be explained as miracles." Jefferson shook his head.

"Like finding Sally at the very time she was needed and using her milk to save baby Jacob?" Adam turned an inquisitive look toward Stephen.

"Exactly." Stephen patted Adam's shoulder. "Think on that miracle if you get discouraged again. I know I shall."

The following morning, they set out on the wagon trail once more girded with refreshed energy and purpose. They skirted around a wagon train with passengers, including several children, who were on their way to Augusta in the Georgia colony at the end of the Great Wagon Road. Stephen spoke with the wagon master, who assured him they would make inquiries of their own of any settlements and towns they passed.

Watching the train move out of sight brought back painful memories for Stephen of the lost souls who had taken part in his journey. He offered a prayer for traveling mercies for this wagon train.

When they finally rode into the trading post yard, they watered and tethered their horses and spread oats they had carried with them.

"You see those four horses there tied to the building posts?" asked Jefferson. "I thought this place would be abandoned."

Reynolds pulled his musket from behind his saddle. "They're Indian horses. Cherokee by the markings on 'em."

"Adam, stay back. Over there behind the horses," Stephen ordered and pulled his pistol from his belt.

The three of them approached the building and stopped at the edge of the porch.

"Who goes there?" Stephen yelled.

"Stephen...Stephen? Is that you?" cried a voice from inside.

The sound of Tessa's voice nearly knocked Stephen to the ground, but when she came running through the doorway, arms flung open wide, he dropped his pistol and ran. He swung her up into his arms. Crying and laughing, she clasped the sides of his head and kissed his forehead, eyelids, cheeks, and finally, his mouth. He matched her kiss for kiss, his heart bursting with joy.

"My darling! It is really you." Tessa threw her arms around him. "I've prayed...I've cried...I've dreamed of this moment."

"As have I." He caressed one of her braids. "Though in my wildest dreams, I never envisioned my beloved running into my arms as an Indian maiden."

"My wonderful new friends gave me these clothes. Are they not beautiful?"

His gaze swept her from head to toe. "Stunning, dear one. Absolutely stunning."

Francis, Doya, and Tala came out and stopped in their tracks at the sight of Tessa and Stephen embracing each other.

"Francis!" Adam shouted as he sped across the yard.

"Brother!"

Holding on tightly to each other, Stephen and Tessa watched the boys hugging and slapping each other on their backs.

Adam stepped back and stared at Francis. "I did not know that I had an Indian brother."

Francis touched the feathers in his topknot. "It's grand, isn't it?"

Adam grinned. "I don't care what you are wearing. I'm so very happy to see you."

Tessa beckoned to the boys, and they all hugged each other in a tight circle.

"We must thank our Lord for this wonderful blessing," Stephen whispered.

They bowed their heads while Stephen offered up a heartfelt prayer of thanksgiving.

Reynolds, who had been watching the intense reunion, wiped a tear from his eye. "That's the nicest thing I ever witnessed in my born days."

Tessa stepped away but kept her arm around Stephen. "This is Doya and Tala. They are scouts for Fort Hampton. They rescued Francis and me and took us to their village until all the fighting stopped."

Stephen bowed first, then offered his hand. "I will never be able to repay what you have done for me and my family."

"We have new family as our payment," Doya said, clasping Stephen's forearm.

Reynolds harrumphed and swung his musket from his right arm to his left. "Let's all go inside. I need to sit down. This has all been a lot to handle."

"Come on, then, you old softy," said Jefferson, who led the way inside.

They gathered on chairs around the tables, except for Tessa, who sat in Stephen's lap. She perused the room and sighed heavily.

"What's the matter, my love?" Stephen tugged playfully on one of her braids.

"All my paintings, my paints, and brushes are gone."

He kissed her cheek. "They are not. They are waiting for you at Fort Hampton."

Her frown turned upside down, and she threw her arms around his neck. "I could burst with happiness. Thank you. Thank you."

Jefferson took a swig from his canteen. "Well, since we're out of a job searching for two people who have come to mean so much to us, what do we do next, Reynolds?"

Doya stood and held out his hands. "Tala and I invite you

all to our village. We will celebrate our new brothers and our coming together."

Reynolds slapped his thigh. "That's a mighty fine idea."

"Please, may we go? You would meet some of the most wonderful people, Stephen," Tessa said. "You could taste their delicious food...listen to their beautiful stories...and we would sleep under the stars..."

Sleeping under the stars with Tessa. A sweet tension flooded Stephen's body.

He toyed with her braid. "Say no more, my love. I'm eager to share something that makes you so happy."

Meeting the Cherokee people Tessa had come to love filled Stephen with eagerness. He also anticipated warning them about an impending war that, according to Colonel Stanton's reckonings, would play out on their lands.

Francis stood and toyed with the beaded bracelet on his wrist. "I'm happy we're going to the village, Stephen, for there is someone I would like very much for you to meet."

What was this? Stephen studied his brother's face and then looked at Tessa, who exchanged a glance with Francis. What secret did his wife and brother share?

"Huzzah!" Adam shouted and headed outside with his arm slung over Francis's shoulder. "Maybe we could find clothes like yours for me."

Francis laughed. "They are the most comfortable I've ever worn. And the Cherokee are the most generous people."

Everyone met outside and readied the horses for the journey.

"Give us a moment?" Stephen asked the others and held Tessa's hand. "I want to show Tessa something."

He guided her to a spot near the edge of the woods and a patch of laurel bushes. "My dearest, I have some news I think may bring you sadness."

He gazed into her beautiful clear blue eyes so full of love for him and regretted what he was about to relay. "I found out when I came here before...when the soldiers were using this place as their headquarters...that Violet was killed when the post was seized."

"Oh, no!" Tessa covered her face with her hands. "If it weren't for her, I don't think we would be alive today."

He gently pulled her hands away. "This is where she was buried, along with many of the outlaws."

She stared at the ground where the grass had started to creep back over the dirt. "No headstone? No markings?"

How Stephen sorely regretted the sorrow in his wife's lovely eyes.

He caressed her cheek. "We will mark her passing in our hearts."

She stiffened her arms to her sides. "And Jared?"

Jared's lost soul had slaked Stephen's thirst for retribution. Pity had replaced revenge.

Stephen ran his fingers up and down her arm. "He was tried for murder, found guilty, and shot by a firing squad."

She blanched. "A fitting punishment for what he did."

"Time to be on our way, Stephen," Francis yelled across the yard.

"Let's go, my darling. So many exciting things await us." He leaned down and nuzzled her ear. "Mm, your hair smells of honeysuckles."

His intimate gesture made her shiver, and he yearned to have her to himself.

Arm in arm, they strolled toward their family and friends and a new life that awaited them.

Stephen tilted her chin to regard her face. "I cannot promise you complete happiness, my Tessa, but know this—I will love you with all my heart until the day we die and beyond. I promise."

EPILOGUE

1793
FORTY YEARS LATER...

Stephen leaned heavily on his cane with his back to the double-door entrance to the building he had purchased on Main Street in Camden, South Carolina.

He scanned the precious faces of his family gathered at the bottom of the steps. His and Tessa's four children, their spouses, and their eight children stood in the center of the group. Francis and his wife, Dustu, their three children, their spouses, and three grandchildren had traveled from their home in the North Carolina mountains.

How could Francis have grandchildren? Where had the time gone?

Francis's youngest grandchild, Adam, the namesake of his great uncle, clung to Dustu's skirts. The bandages on his knees and elbows bore witness that he followed in his great uncle's footsteps.

A vision of his beloved Tessa filled Stephen's mind and tore his heart asunder once again—the pain as crushing as with her passing two years previously.

Stephen braced himself. "You know why we've gathered today—to honor our beloved Tessa and her amazing accomplishments. I purchased this building two years ago, and it has taken me that long to renovate it and to gather as many of her most cherished paintings and sketches as possible."

He motioned for Francis to join him. "I couldn't have done it without Francis's assistance." He clasped his brother's shoulder. "We've invited the public for our first tour tomorrow, but today is our special day as a family. So"—he opened both doors —"without further delay, let us proceed."

Inside, Stephen and Francis stepped aside and waited for everyone to assemble in the grand foyer. A large painting, mounted on an easel and hidden behind a blue silk cloth, dominated the middle of a stage at the end of the room. In the center of the room, on a mahogany table, a huge vase of pink roses filled the air with a sweet aroma. Stephen closed his eyes and breathed in the familiar scent.

Tessa had always favored pink roses after wearing them in her hair for their wedding.

Francis pointed to a stack of pamphlets on the table by the roses. "We have programs to help guide you through the exhibits. Each room opens up to the next and the next in a *U* shape that will lead you back here. We will have refreshments waiting for you."

Adam, Francis's four-year-old grandson, whooped. "Refreshments."

Everyone laughed. Adam resembled his great uncle in more ways than one.

"The first room here to our left holds Tessa's earlier works —the backgrounds she painted with her father."

Three canvases—an Italian palazzo, a Spanish Castillo, and an English country garden—lined the wall on easels. The garden one differed from the others, for Tessa had finished the portrait of Violet on it.

Stephen's oldest daughter joined him and curled her arm through the crook in his elbow. "So this is my namesake. Mother told me the story about Violet when I was a child, but her description didn't do her justice. She was beautiful."

Stephen patted her hand. "We would not have survived without her, Violet. It's fitting that she be featured at the beginning of our story."

Violet and Stephen wandered into the next room accompanied by Violet's fourteen-year-old twin daughters, Patience and Constance.

The twins pointed to the sketch of a cobbler mending a boot and giggled. "He looks so funny, Grandfather."

Stephen smiled. "I thought so, too, when I first saw this sketch. He was one of the passengers on our wagon train. It's where your grandmother and I met."

The memory of the massacre and the mass grave still caused him pain after so many years.

"Oh, look." Constance indicated a sketch. "It's a goat. Grandmother named her Sally."

"Yes. When your grandmother and your Great Uncles Francis and Adam and I were on the wagon trail on our way to Camden, we came across a woman whose husband had fallen down a well. We saved the man, and Sally saved their newborn son, Jacob, by giving her milk."

Constance's eyes grew as big as saucers. "The goat seems so real, I want to touch it."

Violet stepped away to take a closer look at some of the other sketches.

Stephen held hands with the twins. "I received a letter from Jacob, who hopes to visit us this week."

They walked into the next room to find Francis and Dustu gathered with their children and grandchildren.

Sara, their eight-year-old granddaughter, stared at a charcoal sketch. "This is Great Auntie Sara? The one I'm named after?"

"Yes, dear," Dustu replied, twirling a tendril of Sara's jet-black hair.

Sara gently touched the sketch. "But what is it on? It's not paper or canvas."

"The first time your Great Aunt Tessa stayed with us in our village, she was so very excited about drawing a portrait of as many of our tribe as she could. But, she had run out of paper. Our people came up with all manner of substitutes. This one is goat's skin, beaten thin and stiffened."

"Oh, look!" Sara exclaimed. "Here's a drawing of you and grandfather, dressed in Cherokee clothing."

The twins joined their cousins, chattering about which sketches they preferred.

If Stephen had ever harbored any doubts about assembling Tessa's works, the awe and joy they brought to his family assuaged them entirely.

Stephen walked among the others as they slowly made their way through several more rooms with commissioned portraits Tessa had painted over the years. The owners had loaned them to the museum especially for this event.

They came upon a room that featured the largest paintings Tessa had ever done and the smallest.

Dominating one wall was a ten-by-eight-foot portrait of Stephen in his British cavalry officer's uniform. Beside him stood his cherished Knight whom he had lost years previously. His emotions nearly overwhelmed him, and then a delicate hand curled around his.

Abigail, his firstborn's daughter, pressed her shoulder against his. Though he shouldn't, he favored her most among his grandchildren. She had his coloring, dark hair, and pale skin, but she had Tessa's inquisitive crystal-blue eyes. At seventeen, she was already an accomplished artist, who carried draped across her shoulder her grandmother's rucksack. It rarely left her side.

"You look incredibly handsome in your uniform, Grandfather." Abigail smiled up at him. "Grandmother adored you, and she clearly showed it in this painting."

How many others present could make such a profound observance?

He hugged her as they approached the next large painting. In it, he stood between his brothers—Adam in his Continental Army captain's uniform and he and Francis in their militia uniforms.

He could not stop the tears that pooled in his eyes as he sucked in a big breath and let it out slowly. The war with England had changed their lives forever.

Abigail squeezed his hand. "Papa told me that Great Uncle Adam died after the battle right here in Camden."

"Yes, dear. It was 1780. The British won that battle. Adam, an officer in the Continental Army under Baron de Kalb, was taken prisoner and died of measles before I could secure his release." He sighed. "I miss my younger brother more than I can express."

"I know you do, but he's with Grandmother now and our Lord. We will see them again."

Her words flowed as a balm across his tattered heart.

He kissed her cheek. "Now, let me show you a rendering of my mother."

He guided her toward a glass case on a pedestal in the center of the room. He opened the case, removed the cameo, and handed it to Abigail. "This is the original. Tessa made a copy for each of my brothers. Do you see something in it?" He grinned.

"Oh, my! This could be a portrait of me."

Another reason for his partiality.

She placed the brooch back in the case and shut it.

The next room featured portraits of family members—the children and grandchildren as babies, toddlers, and teenagers, and many wedding portraits. Stephen hovered next to the wall as his beloveds shared their joy and laughter.

I miss you, dearest.

A sharp pain lanced his heart, and he pressed his hand to his chest.

Francis stepped close. "It's almost more than I can take in. A lifetime of emotions. Tessa would have loved the family being together like this, but she would have shied clear of the compliments." He clasped Stephen's forearm. "Let's find you a seat, brother."

They entered the foyer, where they sat in two of the chairs circling small tables. The family made their way into the room and headed for the refreshments. His sons, Stephen and William, and his daughters, Violet and Grace, shared an animated conversation about which of the portraits they liked most.

Next to the dessert table, Dustu wiped a handkerchief across the front of grandson Adam's waistcoat already covered in cake icing.

Francis laughed. "We are blessed, are we not, brother?"

"Mightily."

Everyone finished eating and gravitated toward the stage. They grew quiet.

"It's time," said Stephen, who allowed Francis to assist him up the two steps and onto the stage.

They positioned themselves next to the covered painting.

"This gathering has done my heart good. The joy... My cup runneth over. I look out at your dear faces and can't help but see the impression my darling wife had upon each of you." He leaned on his cane. "Many of you are aware of how shy Tessa was about her paintings. She was even more hesitant about her own portrait. I so wanted a likeness of her and asked many times if she would let me commission an artist she approved of. She finally agreed to do a self-portrait." He pressed a hand to his heart. "Before Francis and I unveil it, I want you to know that it's not like any portrait you have ever seen. My precious wife completed it only a few days before she passed. Its meaning is profound and is a testament to Tessa's faith and her love of our Lord Jesus."

He nodded to Francis, and they each clasped the top of the silk cover, pulled it away from the painting, and let it float to the ground.

His audience stood completely still as the aroma of roses wafted across the room.

Violet and Grace held onto each other and began to sob quietly. Others took the hands of or hugged those nearby.

Tessa, dressed in a blue silk gown that billowed around her like a cloud, raced headlong down a wagon road through a dense forest toward a glowing light in the distance. Her long golden tresses, caught up in her urgent pace, flowed around her back. Her pale face, in profile, reflected the distant light.

"Look." Abigail pointed to the painting. "Grandmother is carrying our rucksack."

Stephen held his breath and waited, but not for long.

"The nameplate..." Abigail hesitated. "It says, *Will He let me paint Him?*"

Did you enjoy this book? We hope so!
Would you take a quick minute to leave a review where you purchased the book?
It doesn't have to be long. Just a sentence or two telling what you liked about the story!

Receive a FREE ebook and get updates when new Wild Heart books release: https://wildheartbooks.org/newsletter

Don't miss the next book in the The Great Wagon Road Series!

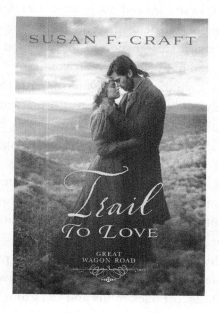

Trail to Love
By Susan F. Craft

1753

Michael Harrigan stepped out of the Pig's Tail tavern and reeled as a blast of torrid air hit him squarely in his face. The heat had not abated even as dusk approached. Someone watching might think him drunk, though he had enjoyed a generous portion of beef pie, cheese, and bread chased with only one tankard of ale. Customarily, he ate a small supper, but he would leave Philadelphia in a few days on a wagon train, and meals akin to the one he had just consumed would not exist on the trail.

He walked off the tavern porch onto the dirt road and headed to the inn where he and his sister-in-law, Megan, and her friend, Amelia, lodged. He had never cared for Megan, especially the way she treated his brother. Cal deserved better. From the moment Michael met Amelia as she disembarked from the ship that had transported the girlhood friends from Scotland, he found her beautiful yet frivolous.

But then, no woman could ever compare to his Heather with her lovely smile, sparkling eyes, and warm, generous nature. He circled his fingertips over his aching heart. Strange how grief slammed into him sometimes as strong as when she had passed. The smallest things triggered his sadness—the smell of roses, an emerald-green dress the same hue as her eyes, the strumming of a mandolin—an instrument she had often played sitting on their front porch—and singing haunting mountains songs.

He shook his head, freeing himself from the painful reverie. Many responsibilities lay ahead, mainly the two women he had been enlisted to escort back to his and Cal's Blue Ridge Mountain home. Amelia and Megan valued their creature comforts, which did not bode well for their three-hundred-mile trek.

Trouble ahead.

The two women had refused to accompany him to what they considered a questionable part of the city and insisted on a meal served to them in their room. The Pig's Tail was near the docks in an area that required caution, but the fare was excellent enough to overcome any concern.

A child's whining echoed through the street. Two blocks down, a young lad yanked on the petticoats of a woman paused on the corner. She jostled a sleeping toddler with one arm and tried to manage the boy with the other. Frowning, she searched one way and then the other.

Farther down the street, a handful of sailors and a couple of ruffians headed her way.

Michael hurried to her side, but she flinched, eyes wide with fear.

He pulled off his tricorn and held it to his chest. "I mean you no harm. This is not a safe place. You are lost?"

Average looking rather than pretty, she reminded him of a wren—brown eyes, brown eyebrows, brown dress. Her mobcap completely covered her hair that was probably the same unremarkable hue as her brows.

Still wary, she took a moment to respond. "This city is like a rabbit warren. I made a wrong turn somewhere, and I can't seem to find my way back." Her pleasing, velvety soft voice held an English accent flavored with a hint of Scottish brogue.

The two groups of men passed around them without commenting, though one of the sailors ogled the woman.

The little boy wrapped his arms around her knees and whimpered.

She rumpled his hair. "David, dear," she coaxed, "please be patient. We'll be home soon."

Her smile brightened her face and lit her eyes. Between it and her comely figure, Michael rethought his first impression of her as plain. Despite their difficulty, the three of them presented a sweet picture. Her husband was a fortunate man.

Michael swept his tricorn to the side and made a slight bow. "I would be happy to escort you. Where are you going?"

Her candid eyes sized him up from head to toe, locking with his own gaze for a moment. He withstood her scrutiny and attempted to maintain an open expression.

Did his frockcoat bear remnants of his meal? Had his cravat remained neatly tied?

Her shoulders relaxed. He had passed muster.

She gave him a tremulous smile. "Applegate Street. We are staying at an inn there."

Her trust warmed him. "I know it. We're staying on that street as well."

The toddler curled on the woman's shoulder wriggled awake and started crying, increasing the frustration on her face.

Michael knelt eye to eye with the young lad attached to her petticoats. "David, is it? How would you like to hop on my shoulders?"

When the boy's eyes lit with delight and he reached up his arms, Michael glanced at the woman. She hesitated a moment and then nodded. He donned his hat and swung David onto his shoulders. The boy dangled his legs on either side of Michael's neck and banged on his tricorn with his fists.

Michael motioned down the street. "This way."

As they wended their way through dirt streets, some no wider than an alleyway, she avoided eye contact and kept a wary distance, constantly glancing at the little boy now clasping his hands around the sides of Michael's beard. The toddler in her arms continued to caterwaul, precluding any communication.

"My dear laddie, do not fash so. Please, will you not calm down? You will make yourself ill." She hiked the child onto her hip and rubbed his back.

How did a body as small as his make such a racket?

Michael maintained their forced silence until they stepped out onto a wide brick-covered thoroughfare.

Someone yelled, "Cleaning!"

Michael gently pushed the woman up against a store wall and positioned himself in front of her moments before gallons of water gushed out of a pump a few yards away. The water shot across the bricks, carrying dirt and debris down the side gullies.

The woman gasped. "What?"

He stepped away from her and the faint aroma of lavender that wafted about her. "They clean the brick streets twice a day. Nice custom, don't you agree?"

"Nice, but surprising."

There it was again, the lovely soft tone of her voice.

They walked another block before she stopped in front of a

two-story clapboard building surrounded by a white picket fence.

The toddler quieted, but not before beads of sweat formed across the woman's brow. She retrieved a handkerchief that was tucked in her under-pocket and dabbed her face. "We're staying here. I can't thank you enough...Mister?"

Michael lowered David to the ground and bowed. "Harrigan. Michael Harrigan."

She jostled the toddler and managed an awkward curtsey. "I'm—"

"Anne! Where have you been?" The question came from a young woman who threw open the gate and stood with her hands jammed onto her hips. Her golden ringlets that curled out from her mobcap bobbed from her irritation. Her blue eyes and creamy skin reminded Michael of the doll he had purchased for his daughter many years ago. "You've had us worried sick!"

"That was *not* my intention, Gail." Flint replaced the velvet in her tone. The ordinary woman with the soft voice had backbone.

"Well, hurry in. We've already begun eating, and we must leave in an hour." She grabbed David's hand, and her mouth twisted into a frown as she finally acknowledged Michael's presence. "You've brought a stranger with you?"

"This is Mr. Harrigan. I became lost, and he was kind enough to help me find my way back."

The blonde made a token curtsy. "You have our gratitude, sir, but we must make haste. Come, Anne. Let's not dawdle."

Anne glanced at him with an apology as she allowed herself to be bustled through the open gate and down the walkway. The color of her expressive eyes—coffee shades with amber flecks—reminded Michael of the white oak acorns so favored by mountain deer.

No, she was definitely not an ordinary woman. Would they

cross paths again? What difference would it make? She was a wife and mother.

He strolled toward his lodgings, preparing his mind for the important meeting ahead.

Throughout their hastily consumed meal and during the entire time Anne changed clothes, her sister-in-law harangued her for getting lost, for putting her sons in danger, and for being late.

Anne tried to explain that she had intended to take the boys out only for a short stroll. They had become unbearably cranky and irritated with their new surroundings and needed fresh air. They had enjoyed playing in a nearby little park until Anne spotted rows of shops that drew her as a bee to nectar. One store sold only bolts of material that filled shelves lined to the ceiling. Another featured buttons, beads, feathers, and embellishments. Anne had never seen so many hanks of thread in one place. She had not taken the boys inside the shops, but had stood before each peering through the windows, her fingers itching to start a new sewing project. It was not long before she became lost.

Overwrought, Gail did not heed Anne's explanation. She was not normally a harridan, though she liked her own way. Anne was hard pressed not to mention that she loved her nephews as if they were her own children and would give her life to keep them safe. During the lecture, Anne's brother, William, wisely found somewhere else to be.

An hour later, after a maid arrived to care for David and Keith, Anne left the inn and, carrying a lantern for their return, took her place behind William and Gail.

Her brother and sister-in-law made an attractive couple. William's sable-brown hair, brown eyes, and dark complexion served as a foil to Gail's porcelain-doll blonde features. Of

medium height, they looked trim in their latest fashions—
Gail's solid blue overskirt and penrose-patterned bodice, and
William's tan breeches and brown waistcoat—all tailored by
Anne. Their handsome appearance made her proud of her
work.

Ahead of them, Mr. Harrigan exited an inn escorting two
women, one on each arm.

Her heart skipped at the sight of him. Why?

The finely dressed women were engaged in a lively conversation. Which one was his wife?

Mr. Harrigan was certainly an attractive man, and his
choice of attire was impeccable. To Anne's tailor's eye, his dove-
gray frockcoat perfectly fit his broad shoulders and trim waist.
Someone very skilled had fashioned his clothing.

Gail frowned at Anne over her shoulder. "Are you certain
about where we are going? Especially in light of what
happened today?"

Anne fought the urge to roll her eyes. "I am. I checked the
map the wagon master left for us at the inn. We follow this
street until it ends at the city boundary and a large field where
the wagons will assemble."

As Anne, William, and Gail neared the city limits, Mr.
Harrigan and his companions headed in the same direction.
Would he be traveling with the wagon train? Anne's arms
tingled.

He answered that question when he guided the women off
the road and across a two-acre field to join a group of people
gathered inside a circle of wagons and tents.

The moment he spotted Anne standing near him, he
regarded William, raised an eyebrow, and then greeted her with
a nod and friendly smile. The smile lit his hazel eyes and crinkled the fine lines at his temples.

Why did he appeal to her? Wasn't he married to one of the

women with him? What difference did it make if he joined the wagon train?

She had made a life for herself caring for her brother's family. She had not thought of love or marriage since her fiancé had passed nine years ago. His death had broken her heart, though the pain had abated over time, and, disturbingly, his visage was becoming a distant memory.

Marriage...children. Was that desire still alive, after all?

ABOUT THE AUTHOR

Susan F. Craft retired after a 45-year career in writing, editing, and communicating in business settings.

She authored the historical romantic suspense trilogy *Women of the American Revolution—The Chamomile, Laurel,* and *Cassia. The Chamomile* and *Cassia* received national Illumination Silver Awards. *The Chamomile* was named by the Southern Independent Booksellers Alliance as an Okra Pick and was nominated for a Christy Award.

She collaborated with the International Long Riders' Guild Academic Foundation to compile *An Equestrian Writer's Guide* (www.lrgaf.org), including almost everything you'd ever want to know about horses.

An admitted history nerd, she enjoys painting, singing,

listening to music, and sitting on her porch watching geese eat her daylilies. She most recently took up the ukulele.

AUTHOR'S NOTES

Camden

Stephen and Tessa head for a settlement, Camden, South Carolina, a real city. Their story takes place in 1753, but at that time, the name of the settlement was Pine Tree Hill. The name was changed in 1768 to Camden to honor Lord Camden, champion of colonial rights.

Explained in the epilogue, my character Adam Griffith is captured during the Revolutionary War at the Battle of Camden, which the British won. The British imprison Adam in a camp where he dies of measles before Stephen can arrange for his release. I based this part of the story on Andrew Jackson and his brother, Robert, who were imprisoned after the Battle of Camden. Reports say they caught either measles or smallpox. Their mother, Elizabeth, arranged for a prisoner swap, but Robert died a few days after returning home.

Fireflies

I based the scene with the parade of fireflies on the synchronous fireflies my husband and I saw when we stayed in the Blue Ridge Mountains many years ago. What an amazing phenomenon! Every year between mid-May and mid-June, the Congaree National Park in Hopkins, South Carolina, near my home, hosts a synchronous fireflies event. For more information, see the blog I wrote about it:

http://historicalfictionalightintime.blogspot.com/2017/03/synchronized-fireflies-awesome.html

Goat Hide Canvas

The Cherokee gift Tessa with goat leather to use as canvas. Traditionally called Moroccan leather, it is considered one of the finest leathers in the world. Since Shakespearean times, goat leather was used for bookbinding. It is known for its softness, flexibility, and strength.

Limners

By the early 1700s, wealthy families hired painters, referred to as "limners," to paint portraits of their families. Limners were among the first to record glimpses of life in Colonial America.

These limners, mostly self-taught, generally unknown by name, turned out portraits in the Elizabethan style, the Dutch baroque style, or the English baroque court style, depending upon the European background of both artist and patron. Many limners painted miniatures—tiny watercolor portraits—on pieces of ivory, often oval-shaped, commonly worn as jewelry.

If you're interested in more information, I wrote a blog about Colonial limners that can be found on the Colonial Quills blogspot:

https://colonialquills.blogspot.com/2013/05/limners-colonial-american-portrait.html

Paint

In my research, I discovered that long before tubes, early

artists kept their mixed-oil paints fresh by storing them in pig bladders. To retrieve the paint, they would poke holes in the bladders with needles or sharpened bones. While researching, I also discovered that Leonardo da Vinci preferred using walnut oil over turpentine and linseed oil to thin his paints and to clean his brushes.

Royal Regiment of Horse Guards (The Blues)

Stephen was a soldier in the Royal Regiment of Horse Guards, also known as The Blues. When he purchased his commission at the age of seventeen, he may have been too young to fight in the Battle of Dettingen in June 1743, where one of The Blues rescued King George II and the Household Cavalry Brigade was formed. The Battle of Mumbai mentioned in the novel is fictitious, but I based it on a 1745 battle in France where cannon ripped through The Blues, causing terrible damage.

Violet

I wanted Violet to have purple eyes, so in my research I discovered that lavender or purple eyes are genetic traits of albinism. Therefore, I made Violet's mother have that trait. I also discovered that, in the eyes of the Cherokee, purple is a symbol of wisdom. Due to its associations with animals and death, purple was never employed in their face or body painting.

I offer my sincere appreciation to the Oconaluftee Indian Village in Cherokee, North Carolina. They have recreated a 1760s village with traditional dwellings, work areas, and sacred ritual places. During the numerous times I visited the village, the sights, sounds, and smells enthralled me. I witnessed the people making a canoe, sculpting pottery, hand-fashioning beadwork, weaving cane baskets, and forming thistle into darts for a blowgun. As a history nerd, I could not have been happier.

I also thank the Cherokee Nation for the fabulous videos, "Cherokee Word of the Week," where Cherokee words are spoken, spelled out, and defined. The site helped me create names for my Cherokee characters.

Thank you to Ghost Farmer Productions and the Museum of History NSW for the video "Loading and Firing a Musket in 1776."

And, of course, I extend heartfelt gratitude to my Lord from who all blessings flow.

Soli Deo Gloria.

If you love historical romance, check out the other Wild Heart books!

Texas Forsaken by Sherry Shindelar
The man who destroyed her life may be the only one who can save it.

Seven years ago, Maggie Logan (Eyes-Like-Sky) lost everything she knew when a raid on a wagon train tore her from her family. As the memories of her past faded to nothing more than vague shadows, Maggie adapted, marrying a Comanche warrior, having a baby, and rebuilding her life. But in one terrible battle, the U.S. Cavalry destroys that life and she is taken captive again, this time by those who call themselves her people. Forced into a world she wants nothing to do with, Eyes-

Like-Sky's only hope at protecting her child may be an engagement to the man who killed her husband.

Enrolled in West Point to escape his overbearing father, Captain Garret Ramsey finds himself assigned to the Texas frontier, witnessing the brutal Indian War in which both sides commit atrocities. Plagued by guilt for his own role, Garret seeks redemption by taking responsibility for the woman he widowed and her baby. Though he is determined to do whatever it takes to protect them, is he willing to risk everything for a woman whose heart is buried in a grave?

~

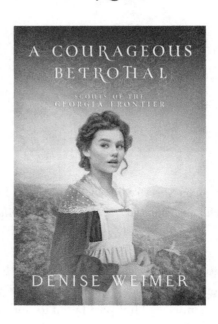

A Courageous Betrothal by Denise Weimer

A *wounded lieutenant*, *a woman fierce enough to protect her family*, and an American Revolution with everything at stake.

Red-haired, freckle-faced, and almost six feet tall, Jenny White has resigned herself to fame over love. Possessing the courage and wits to guard her younger siblings against nature, natives, and loyalists in Georgia's "Hornet's Nest" gives life meaning until she meets scout Caylan McIntosh.

From the time Jenny nurses the young lieutenant back to health after the Battle of Kettle Creek, she can't deny her attraction to the vexing Highlander, who seems determined to dismantle her emotional armor. But when Georgia falls to the British and Caylan returns to guide Jenny's family on a harrowing exodus into the North Carolina mountains, will his secrets prove stronger than his devotion? Or will their love be courageous enough to carry them through the battles ahead?

~

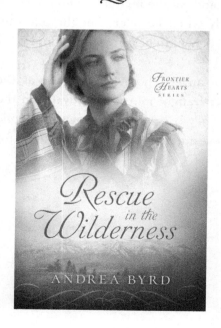

Rescue in the Wilderness by Andrea Byrd

William Cole cannot forget the cruel burden he carries, not with the pock marks that serve as an outward reminder. Riddled with guilt, he assumed the solitary life of a long hunter, traveling into the wilds of Kentucky each year. But his quiet existence is changed in an instant when, sitting in a tavern, he overhears a man offering his daughter—and her virtue—to the winner of the next round of cards. William's integrity and desire for redemption will not allow him to sit idly by while such an injustice occurs.

Lucinda Gillespie has suffered from an inexplicable illness her entire life. Her father, embarrassed by her condition, has subjected her to a lonely existence of abuse and confinement. But faced with the ultimate betrayal on the eve of her eighteenth birthday, Lucinda quickly realizes her trust is better placed in his hands of the mysterious man who appears at her door. Especially when he offers her the one thing she never thought would be within her grasp—freedom.

In the blink of an eye, both lives change as they begin the difficult, danger-fraught journey westward on the Wilderness Trail. But can they overcome their own perceptions of themselves to find love and the life God created them for?

Made in the USA
Monee, IL
29 September 2024

66796720R10128